RAINBOW
OVER HELL

RAINBOW
OVER HELL

he death row deliverance of a World War II assassin

Tsuneyuki Mohri
Translated by Sharon Fujimoto-Johnson

Pacific Press® Publishing Association
Nampa, Idaho
Oshawa, Ontario, Canada
www.pacificpress.com

Book designed by Eucaris L. Galicia
Cover art by GettyImages.com

Originally published in Japanese as *Jigoku-no Niji* in 1998 by Mainichi
Newspapers Company and in 2005 by Kodansha Publishing Company

Additional copies of this book are available by calling toll free
1-800-765-6955 or visiting AdventistBookCenter.com

Library of Congress Cataloging-in-Publication data:

ISBN: 0-8163-2134-5
ISBN13: 9780816321346

06 07 08 09 10 • 5 4 3 2 1

Acknowledgments

The author and translator would like to express their gratitude to the following individuals for their efforts toward, and encouragement of, the translation of this book: Dr. Masao Kunihiro, Yoshika Caraig, Hitomi Johnson, Dr. Edward and Karen Fujimoto, Kikue Fujimoto, Yuki and Yumiko Fujita, Shinsei Hokama, Masaji Uyeda, Tadaomi Shinmyo, Toshio Yamagata (deceased), Mikuni Terui, Dr. Dennis M. Ogawa, and Jeremy Fujimoto-Johnson. They would also like to give special thanks to editors Russ Holt and Tim Lale and publicist Nicole Batten of Pacific Press, as well as the staff of Pacific Press, for their efforts in making this work available to English-language readers.

Contents

Chapter 1

The Journey Begins

Yasufumi Miike stole a glance at the man sitting quietly in the window seat beside him on the left side of the Boeing 727. The casual, open-necked shirt did little to identify Pastor Saburo Arakaki as a man of the cloth. Nor did his sturdy, large-boned physique, robust arms, and tanned forehead. His large black eyes were gentle but, from time to time, took on a piercing light. The scar on his lower right jaw resembled something received in a bar fight but actually had been caused by a bullet. He had already celebrated his sixtieth birthday, but absolutely nothing in his expression or the way he carried himself betrayed his age.

He briefly exchanged small talk with Miike, then soon turned and stared out the window. Continental-Micronesia Flight 974, from Fukuoka to Saipan, continued its steady course toward the gleaming morning sunlight. Far below, the horizon drew an endless faint arc between sky and sea. In the seat beside Pastor Arakaki, Miike felt wonder and apprehension mingle deep in his heart. The long-awaited journey had begun, at last. *But,* he wondered, *was it the right thing to do?*

In 1945, Pastor Arakaki—a teenager at that time—had committed two murders in Saipan and had been sentenced to death. After nine years in prison, his life was miraculously extended—and transformed. He had become, of all things, a preacher of the gospel! What had transformed a convicted murderer into a preacher? Miike wanted to know.

This journey would trace Pastor Saburo Arakaki's past. A TV film crew accompanied the two. Pastor Arakaki had consented to the trip, of course. Nonetheless, to have his dark past exposed before the eye of a camera . . .

the trip could become unconscionably difficult. A sense of uneasiness underlay everything. In spite of it, Miike was in rather a good mood; the logistics for the trip had mysteriously fallen into place almost as if someone were guiding events.

It had all begun a month earlier.

Late one night, Miike had entered a hotel on the bank of Nakagawa River in Fukuoka. Until two days earlier, he had been working on location at Ayukawa Bay in the town of Oshika, reporting on the plight of whaling ships facing closure of their coastal operations due to worldwide antiwhaling sentiment. Now he was in Fukuoka for a planning session for a television program.

The evening edition of the *Mainichi Shinbun* was in the hotel room when he returned. Miike flipped through the pages, uninterested even by the headlines, when suddenly a small article caught his eye. It read:

Former Death Row Convict, Pastor Arakaki, Preaches On
Because it is indeed an "Age of Dark Premonitions"

Mr. Saburo Arakaki (61) of Naha City, who has followed an odd destiny from death row convict to preacher, after he murdered two Japanese leaders for cooperating with U. S. troops in a Saipan civilian detention camp, lectured for four days in Kokura City in northern Kyushu.

The impact of the tantalizingly short article brought Miike to his feet. He wanted to hear this man's lecture! It wasn't the first time he had read an article about Mr. Saburo Arakaki. In fact, a few years earlier, while working on a television program dealing with religion, Miike had come across several articles about Pastor Arakaki's lectures. Miike's work on the religion-related TV program at the time had caused him to think about God's existence. Now, he clipped the article from the newspaper that lay spread across his hotel bed. *I'd really like to meet that man,* he said to himself.

He was familiar with an outline of Arakaki's past. He knew that Arakaki had been one of those zealous, militaristic youths in Saipan, the so-

called *gunkoku shonen,* and that he had helped the Japanese army in guerilla activities after U.S. armed forces landed on the island toward the end
of World War II. He knew that Arakaki had then surrendered in order to
infiltrate a civilian detention camp and that, on the orders of a Japanese
MP, he had assassinated two Japanese detainees who were cooperating with
the U.S. military. He knew that Arakaki was subsequently sentenced to
death at a military trial and spent terror-filled days awaiting execution following his transfer to Guam. There the death sentence had been commuted
to life imprisonment in Hawaii. And in Hawaii, Arakaki encountered the
Bible. Its teachings penetrated his heart. He searched his soul and reflected
on his crime—double murder. He received a special pardon, was eventually released from prison, and had become a preacher. . . .

Could all this have actually happened in real life? Miike wondered. *Could
it really be?* He felt a quivering in his soul.

Born in 1933, Miike was in his first year of middle school, under the old
educational system, when the war ended. He, too, had been a zealous
gunkoku shonen, or militaristic youth, and had harbored aspirations of becoming a military pilot. With Japan's defeat, times changed drastically for
him and others.

Even after Miike became involved in broadcast dramas and documentaries, his interest in the war remained strong. In fact, his first piece to be
broadcast nationwide (in 1961 when he was twenty-seven) was a television
drama of the death sentence of a twenty-seven-year-old army lieutenant
and POW concentration camp chief who was held responsible for POW
slayings and tried by the Eighth U.S. military court in Yokohama. This
man became the first to be sentenced at the Sugamo prison trials for war
crimes.

Miike was born into a family that belonged to the Buddhist "Jodo" sect;
his grandmother was a particularly fervent believer. That didn't necessarily
mean that Miike himself believed in Buddhism. Around the time of his
graduation from college, he had a slight brush with Christianity. He dili-
gently read through a Bible correspondence course, but when faced with
the question, "Do you believe that Jesus Christ is the Son of God?" he
found himself unable to answer "Yes." But in the various experiences of life

during the years that followed, Miike had come to believe that an invisible, higher power did exist.

The morning after seeing the newspaper article about Pastor Arakaki, Miike met with Shun Ejima, the assistant director of TV production at Kyushu Asahi Broadcasting Company. The two men had collaborated on documentaries and shared similar viewpoints on many issues. Without a word, Miike handed the newspaper clipping to Ejima. Ejima skimmed through the article. Then he nodded; he understood.

"I'd really like to try to meet Mr. Arakaki. Maybe we can come up with something," Miike said.

That afternoon, Ejima reported that there were thirteen people by the name of Saburo Arakaki listed in the telephone book for Naha City, but that he had finally found the right one.

"Miike-san, let's start planning a documentary. I'd like for you to meet with Mr. Arakaki right away."

"A documentary?"

"Yes. Perhaps Mr. Arakaki will agree. Would you please ask him?" It was an unexpected development.

Pastor Arakaki's home in Naha City, Okinawa, turned out to be a small church with a sign that read "Oroku Seventh-day Adventist Church." The Seventh-day Adventist Church, Miike had learned, is a Protestant Christian denomination that believes in the second coming of Christ, obeys the Ten Commandments, and keeps Saturday holy as the Sabbath.

The building served as both Pastor Arakaki's church and his home. A worship hall had been set up on the second floor. The pastor greeted Miike and his associates at the door, dressed casually in everyday clothes. He seemed, to Miike, to be an honest, unsophisticated man.

The pastor guided them into the traditional Japanese-style room next to the worship hall, and after they had exchanged pleasantries, Miike shifted in his seat and said, "You have an amazing story—from a death row convict to a preacher! I heard about your story, and I had to find out more."

Pastor Arakaki nodded.

"The transformation in your heart in Saipan, in Guam, in Hawaii—and how these things happened . . . I'm intrigued by it all."

"I see."

"I produce documentaries. I thought we could make a trip tracing the course of your life."

"A trip?"

"Yes, with you."

Silence.

"I want to see what it's like there now. What if we visited the actual sites—Saipan, Guam, Hawaii? Something amazing happened in your heart there. Please, share your story with us there on site." At the time, Miike didn't realize what a cruel request he was making. After all, Pastor Arakaki had often spoken about his past at public seminars; Miike felt sure the pastor would agree to cooperate with the documentary. He plowed forward.

"I want to share your miraculous experiences with the world. I think this story will affect viewers in a very positive way."

The pastor looked at Miike intently. His eyes seemed to pierce straight through to his heart. *He must be wondering if he can trust me,* Miike thought. *And with good reason. I don't know who or what God is. I'm not even a Christian. TV doesn't always take the truth and communicate it accurately. Even in this case, it would be easy to treat the truth as a trifling matter. The story could be communicated carelessly, packaged for entertainment, misrepresented to the world. He must be thinking that he has no guarantee that the documentary will protect his character and deserve his trust.*

All Miike could do was simply to let things be.

"Will you tell the truth?" Pastor Arakaki finally spoke. A fierce light shone in his eyes as he looked squarely into Miike's face.

"Yes," Miike answered. *Reporting without distorting the truth—I think we can promise that,* he thought.

The pastor closed his eyes and lowered his head. For a long moment, he was silent and motionless. Then he looked up and said, "Those are the places where I did such horrible things. . . . Where my life was overturned. If there really is an opportunity to tell the truth. . . . Let's do it!"

"So you'll go?"

Pastor Arakaki nodded quietly.

Over the next three days, Miike listened to Pastor Arakaki recount his story: his upbringing in Okinawa, the tragic events that followed, his conversion, and how he became a pastor. Miike took careful notes, feeling deeply moved all the while.

Producer Ejima immediately launched plans for a program, titled *Testament: A Journey of Confession.* Kyushu Asahi Broadcasting Company decided to begin production immediately on the one-hour documentary. Miike was appointed to accompany Pastor Arakaki on a trip to Saipan, Guam, and Hawaii. His role in the documentary would be the listener in the story. He, together with director Shigemitsu Imura and a camera and audio crew, would depart for Saipan in only a month!

Now, in the Saipan-bound airplane, Miike watched Pastor Arakaki stare out the window. A mysterious and incomprehensible emotion filled him; a sense of responsibility. What would the trip bring forth? He didn't know, but he felt sure it would be something that would affect all of them.

For one . . . two . . . three hours, the Boeing 727 flew onward—toward Saipan, the island of forty-two-year-old bitter experiences.

Chapter 2

Leaving Home

Saburo Arakaki was born on April 24, 1926, as the oldest son of a farming family in the Kagamizu section of Oroku-Son, a village on the main island of Okinawa. Two younger sisters and a little brother joined the family later.

Today, Kagamizu is close to the Naha airport terminal. When Saburo was a boy, it was a small colony consisting of vegetable plots and potato fields strung along the base of a terrace facing the East China Sea. The area is famous for the Kagamizu radish, the best in Okinawa. Saburo's family, however, lived in poverty. Meals consisted mainly of sweet potatoes and an occasional fish from the sea. Rice was a delicacy tasted only at New Year's and during the summer O-Bon festival. If typhoons or droughts struck the area and the harvest was poor, even sweet potatoes were scarce.

Saburo's father, who had a small sugarcane farm, was heavily burdened by debt. No matter how hard he worked, the debts seemed to pile up higher and higher. Once, when Saburo was six and Father had gone out for the day, a moneylender arrived at the door, his face red with rage. He shouted angrily at Saburo's mother and grandmother. "Where did that good-for-nothing husband of yours run away to? I'm telling you, I want my money back! Come on now; hand it over!"

Mother threw herself prostrate on the ground, begging and stalling for time. The man refused to listen to her pleas and began to seize whatever was within reach. Mother desperately clung to his arm. He shook her off brutally, slamming her head over heels against a wall.

"Mama!" Saburo's sisters began to scream.

"You devil!" Grandmother shouted. In return, the man struck her cheek. Thrown off her feet, Grandmother staggered and toppled over. Impulsively, Saburo leaped out from where he had been watching behind a torn shoji screen. He sank his teeth in the man's hairy arm.

"Ow! Get off me, you brat!" The man knocked Saburo in the head with all his strength. Saburo doubled over in pain and fell headfirst onto the floor.

"You good-for-nothing bunch of losers!" With parting curses, the moneylender left Saburo crumpled on the floor, crying in frustration.

Shortly afterwards, Father left for Tinian, a small island located about five miles (eight kilometers) southwest of Saipan in the Northern Marianas island chain. He had heard that the Nanyo Kohatsu Company there paid tenant sugarcane farmers well, but the money he sent home was not much. More loans were negotiated, and the angry moneylender continued to arrive like clockwork when the family couldn't make the necessary payments. Saburo had to watch his mother endure more beatings. He couldn't bear her tears, so as soon as possible he began doing odd jobs around the neighborhood earning a *sen* or two, which he brought home to his mother.

When Saburo was old enough to enter elementary school, an aunt arranged for some distant farming relatives to take him in. In exchange for meals, Saburo helped with chores such as baby-sitting, carrying water, and cutting hay for the cattle. The daily physical labor gave him a sturdy physique. The most difficult task, for seven-year-old Saburo, was hauling night soil. With the man of the house, Saburo would go to the red-light district of Naha City to remove excrement from the bathrooms, dump it into buckets, and haul it back to the farm by cart. If they ran into anyone they knew from the village, it was a disaster. The villagers would jeer at the stench; some even threw stones. Saburo learned to ignore them. Pressing his lips tightly, he silently pulled the cart.

Even at school, Saburo's classmates gathered around to taunt him. "Hey, man, you reek! *Oink, oink! Oink, oink!"* The teasing escalated into bullying. It was always the same—one gave him a little push; then the others descended on him, kicking.

Saburo patiently endured it at first, but he reached his limit the day he was kicked in the groin. Nearly choking from the intense pain, he let his bottled anger explode. Furiously, he gave his opponent a blow to the head. Instantly, the confrontation became a brawl, and he soon knocked down three of his tormentors. A fourth was bleeding from the nose and whimpering. The rest were fleeing from Saburo's desperate rage.

After that incident, no one dared to tease or harass him. Everyone was scared of Saburo's fury and sheer strength whenever he lost his temper. The bullies turned on others who were weaker, and these ran to Saburo for protection. At the risk of making things worse for himself, Saburo fought with all his strength for those who were weaker than he. Before long, everyone wanted to be on his side, and Saburo had become the popular leader of the kids in the neighborhood.

Sometimes, when there was a lot of work to do on the farm, Saburo was not allowed to go to school. During the sugar-refining season, he had to get out of bed before daybreak to work at the refinery. There he walked behind the workhorses that circled the sugarcane press, whipping them around and around until the day finally ended. As a result, he failed the second grade because he hadn't attended enough days.

During his second attempt at the second grade, Saburo learned that his mother had vanished. Rumors flew. It was said that she had run away with a man. "Your mama . . . she ran away with her lover, I heard. *Ha, ha!*" an older boy taunted. Without a word, Saburo knocked him to the ground.

That evening, all alone, eight-year-old Saburo climbed the hill behind his home and stood gazing at the sea. The water moved with the flow of the Japanese Kuroshio current, and the waves were stained by the colors of the setting sun. He resented his mother who had abandoned him and his siblings. The sun set, and as he sat staring up at the stars in the night sky, his resentment toward his mother turned to sorrow; he let the tears flow. Mother couldn't bear all her misery, thought eight-year-old Saburo in his young heart.

When Mother abandoned Saburo, along with his brother and sisters, Grandmother was at her wit's end. She was old and unable to work to feed all the children. There were simply too many mouths to feed. Finally, some relatives arranged for another family to take care of Saburo's sisters; the girls were led away sobbing, and the family was scattered all across the countryside.

During the New Year holiday of Saburo's eighth year, a former resident of Oroku returned from Tinian saying that Saburo's father had asked him to bring Saburo back with him to Tinian. Father had heard of his family's plight and had decided that he could, at least, send for Saburo. He intended, somehow, to send his oldest son to the Saipan Vocational School. He wanted to give Saburo the chance to someday work in Tinian. He knew firsthand what it meant to be uneducated.

Saburo, however, didn't want to go to Tinian, a faraway island in the Pacific that he had only heard of. He was afraid—afraid of leaving Japan, afraid of leaving his sisters. Nonetheless, the adults had made the decision; he would go to Tinian. Saburo had hardly any belongings, so packing to leave was not a problem. He visited his sisters and said his goodbyes. "You take care of yourselves, now. And take care of Grandma, too," he told them.

"Good luck, big brother!" they cried. Saburo bit his lip. He was determined not to let them see his tears.

I might never see them again, the thought flashed through his mind. And just as quickly came the desire: *I wish I could see my mother.* However much he might wish to see her again, he knew it was useless. There was no chance of finding his mother, even if he searched for her.

In March 1934, Saburo left Okinawa. It was a lonesome departure. First, he had to get to Yokohama to board a ship that would take him to Tinian. So along with the man whom his father had sent to get him, Saburo boarded a Ryukyu Kaiun shipping steamship from Naha Bay on the first leg of his journey. The Kuroshio Sea was rough in early spring, and it was his first sea journey. He couldn't stop vomiting. The man from Tinian ignored Saburo as much as possible, spending his time with some acquaintances he made on the ship and drinking brandy. Even in the middle of the day he was often drunk.

After docking at Kagoshima in Kyushu, Saburo boarded a train for the first time in his life. He and the man headed for Moji on the Kagoshima

Honsen, the main line. Saburo drank in the sight of the mainland towns and villages as they surged by outside the window. His eyes widened at the sheer size of the mountains and rivers—gigantic compared to what he had seen in Okinawa. Then the train suddenly entered a tunnel, and Saburo leaped out of his seat. Everything he saw and heard was new and shocking. It was enough to make him dizzy.

They crossed the Kanmon strait by ferry and then once again caught a train on the Sanyo Honsen line. After traveling all day and through the night, they reached Yokohama at last.

Saburo was shivering. The cold, salty wind pierced his skin. Nevertheless, before the ship left port, he stood alone on the deck gazing out over the harbor scene as if he couldn't get enough of it. Ships of all sizes jostled together in Yokohama Harbor, and the docks bustled with life. The foreign flags that flew from the ships' masts, the colorful array of buildings that dotted the harbor, the cars coming and going, the people walking in the park—everything seemed fascinating to Saburo's eyes. *This is goodbye to Japan, I guess,* he thought as he gazed out over his motherland.

"Hey, you'll catch a cold, dressed like that!" a crew member called out.

It was early spring, barely the beginning of March, and Saburo didn't even have a coat; he was dressed for summer in short pants, and even those were threadbare. All that belonged to him was bundled up in a single *furoshiki* cloth.

His face to the wind, Saburo stood on the deck. He had prominent, dignified eyebrows and large black eyes that darted about, filled with anxiety and a wild light that failed to cloak his curiosity.

When the loading of the Tinian/Saipan-bound ship was completed, a gong sounded, and the ship's whistle made the harbor air tremble. Ribbons fluttered in the air between the ship's passengers and those on the wharf waiting to see them off. Of course, no one was there to see Saburo off as the ship pulled away from the pier.

From Okinawa to Tinian, by way of Yokohama, Saburo traveled twenty-five hundred miles (four thousand kilometers) to reach his laborer father. Left far behind him were his impoverished, weeping grandmother, brother, and sisters. He bit his lip, determined to endure the miserable situation.

Heading straight for Saipan, the cargo-passenger ship sailed some twelve hundred miles (two thousand kilometers) south. As it passed Hachijo-jima Island, rough waves began to rock the ship, and Saburo became violently ill. When he wasn't vomiting, he lay on the *tatami* mats in his third-class cabin, his body sliding across the floor as the ship swayed. Giant waves crashed onto the side of the ship, and the engine echoed in Saburo's sleep-deprived body. He thought he would surely lose his mind.

Eventually, the sea calmed, and Saburo's seasickness subsided enough for him to go out on the lower deck. The light was dazzling. The sky was clear, and the wind was mildly warm. It was like spring in Okinawa. Stretching out both arms, Saburo took a deep breath. He felt much better. He climbed up to the upper deck. Looking all around, he saw that the blue of the ocean stretched in all directions as far as he could see.

Day after day, the ship sailed across the plains of the ocean. The wind that teased young Saburo's cheeks became increasingly warm, and rain clouds billowed in the sky ahead. Saburo remembered how he used to swim among the coral reefs off of Okinawa, and he began once again to feel like the boy who was the popular leader of the kids in his neighborhood. His mischievous spirit returned; with youthful agility, he tore up and down the stairs, exploring the ship.

"Hey, kid, come over here, and I'll show you something neat," someone called. A crew member was offering to show him the engine room. Saburo's mouth dropped open in disbelief when he saw the enormity of the roaring engine. The engine room crew laughed as Saburo shouted in excitement. He was a good kid without a trace of bad intentions—and friendly, too. The crew members all looked after him affectionately.

After several days at sea the sun shone so strongly that its reflection off the water hurt Saburo's eyes, and the breeze that blew across the deck felt like a summer wind. One day Saburo stood on the upper deck looking in all directions. Suddenly he saw the outline of an island ahead. "Hey!" he shouted to no one in particular, "there's an island!"

"That's Saipan," a crew member explained. "See, right beyond it is Tinian."

Father is waiting there. In just a little while, I'll see him. An image of the often-tortured look on his father's face slipped into Saburo's mind. *What will I say when I see him?* Something that couldn't be put into words flooded Saburo's heart and moved him to tears.

The ship entered Tanapag Harbor on Saipan's western shore and headed toward the pier. Sounds of activity wafted out from the city of Garapan, known as the Tokyo of the South Sea. Disembarking passengers gathered near the gangway, carrying their luggage. Saburo stood alone on the upper deck looking over the city—the shopping district and the rows of houses standing side by side. Red-roofed buildings. A Spanish-style church. In the distance the giant chimneys of the sugar refinery. The green of coconut palm leaves. White-sand beaches. The scenery of the tropical island was even more colorful than Okinawa.

Looking upward, Saburo saw a rainbow draped across the sky; its magnificent arch straddled the facing mountain.

"That's Mount Tapotchau, the tallest mountain on the island," a crew member told Saburo.

"Tapotchau?" He felt as though the rainbow hanging over the mountain with the funny-sounding name was welcoming him. Eight-year-old Saburo couldn't know that these islands, known as the South Sea Paradise, would someday become a battlefield hell and force him to stand on a precipice of terror and despair.

But the seeds of war had already been planted. Three years earlier, in 1931, Japanese troops had landed on Chinese territory, taking advantage of the Manchurian Incident and spreading combat wherever they went. Japan was trampling into a bog of what would turn out to be fifteen years of war—between Japan and China, and later, the Pacific war with the United States and its allies.

Chapter 3

War Comes to Saipan

The Boeing 727 began reducing altitude as it approached Saipan. "Look, we're starting to be able to see Mount Tapotchau now," Pastor Arakaki pointed out the window. Yasufumi Miike peered out.

A long, thin island, stretching north and south, floated in the Prussian blue Micronesian waters. It was a tiny island, smaller even than Tanegashima in Kagoshima. They could also see the cliffs on the northern cape and the white-crested waves that shattered themselves against it. Miike saw Pastor Arakaki's eyes darken for a fleeting moment.

In 1944, this island had been a battleground of fierce combat during the Pacific war; nearly fifty thousand Japanese soldiers and civilians died by gunfire or honorable suicide for Japan.

* * * * *

The Pacific war started with a triumphant Japan and the surprise attack on Pearl Harbor on December 7, 1941. But by June of the following year, the war had turned around, triggered by the major defeat of the combined fleet of the Japanese navy in the Battle of Midway. The retaliation of the U.S. army resulted in an intensifying series of defeats for Japanese troops—in the Solomon Islands, Guadalcanal, Tawara in the Gilbert Islands; the suicide of the Makin Island defense forces, and the loss, one after the other, of the Marshall Islands, Kwajalein, and Rota Island. At the battle front in Burma, the Imphal campaign resulted in a crushing defeat for Japan. Powerful U.S. forces overthrew the Japanese troops in New Guinea. Plowing westward, the U.S. forces under General MacArthur had an eye on retaking the Philippines.

For the Japanese Imperial Headquarters, Saipan was strategically positioned in the Pacific Ocean on the edge of the radius absolutely necessary for safeguarding Japanese territory. Hideki Tojo—who held concurrently the positions of prime minister, minister of war, and chief of staff—reported to the emperor that Saipan was, in effect, impregnable. Saipan became the "bulwark of the Pacific Ocean."

At the same time, the U.S. forces were planning to take over Saipan, Tinian, and the surrounding islands. They wanted to use the islands as a strategic base from which to launch air raids on the Japanese homeland to deplete her military power with their newest far-ranging bomber, the B-29 called the Super Fortress.

June 1944. Around a nucleus of 15 American aircraft carriers bearing 891 planes, U.S. Task Force Fifty-eight advanced toward Saipan from the southeast. Shielded in the rear by battleships, cruisers, and destroyers, the massive transport fleet of the Fifth Amphibious Corps followed. It was an enormous invading force made up of a total of 775 vessels.

At that time, Saburo Arakaki was spending the last of his school days as a third-year student in the agriculture department of the Saipan Vocational School. He had just turned eighteen. Ten years had past since he had left Okinawa to live with his father in Tinian.

Saipan Vocational School in Garapan, at the center of the island of Saipan, was the only vocational school established by the government in the South Sea Islands under Japan's rule. During wartime, uniforms became national defense khakis, school caps were exchanged for military helmets, and students tied girdles around their waists and walked to school in *tabi,* split-toed, rubber-soled socks.

Just as in Japan itself, military education was hammered into the students on Saipan, and much of class time was dedicated to military training. In Okinawa, where Saburo had been born and raised, worship of the emperor had been advanced ever since the so-called disposal of the Ryukyus, at the beginning of Meiji Period when the Ryukyu monarchy had become Okinawa Prefecture. To live as the child of His Imperial Highness and to be willing even to give up one's life to protect the Divine Nation, Japan, was proof of being Japanese.

The immortality of the Divine Nation was likewise taught at the Saipan Vocational School, and Saburo and his classmates were trained to be ready to take up their arms and fight on the battlefield to exterminate "the savage Americans and British."

At the end of 1943, military veterans had begun to be drafted into the army. Military exercises intensified in the youth corps, volunteer squads, and women's national defense societies. Bomb shelters were dug all over the island.

In February 1944, Saipan suffered the first U.S. military air raid. After that, reconnaissance planes flew overhead continually. Even young Saburo felt it in his bones—war clouds were gathering.

The Imperial Headquarters hastily dispatched additional troops and attempted to strengthen the island's defenses with the Forty-third Division of the Thirty-first Army and the Forty-seventh Independent Combined Brigade. However, U.S. submarines sank many transport ships. Those soldiers who narrowly managed to escape drowning and made it to shore were completely unarmed, carrying nothing but the clothes on their backs. Of the forty-two thousand army and navy troops, slightly less than half survived, with no fighting capacity.

Saipan is a long, narrow island, measuring nearly twenty miles (19.2 kilometers) north to south and from 1.5 to 6 miles (2.4 to 9.6 kilometers) east to west. Here and there, in unexpected places, defense barricades were constructed.

Saburo had been living in the school dormitory, but in April the army took over both the school building and the dorm, so he had no choice but to find other lodging. Classes were no longer held regularly. Saburo and his classmates were sent out daily with the labor mobilization troops to construct fortifications.

Occasionally, as Saburo worked on the farm grounds or in the fields among the smell of dirt and grass cuttings, he thought of his father in Tinian. Saburo's father always smelled of sweat. As a tenant farmer, he slaved away on the sugarcane fields of the South Sea Development Company. He was continually on the move, searching for land that might bring even a little more profit. As a result, Saburo had changed schools countless times—Marupo Elementary School, Hagoi Elementary School, Sonson Advanced Primary School. Besides going to school, he had helped his father in the cane fields. Upon returning home, they had to carry out the tasks—cooking, laundry, and cleaning—that a housewife might have done.

Saburo's father's overriding thought was to get Saburo into the Saipan Vocational School. Day after day he would nag and shout at Saburo to study, study, study. A taciturn man who was not good with words, Saburo's father didn't know any other way to put it. Saburo, on the other hand, wanted to have fun.

During the time that he attended Sonson Advanced Primary School, Saburo was defiant toward his father, and there were nights when he didn't come home. The "neighborhood leader of the kids" in Okinawa was no different in Tinian, and Saburo let his wild reputation run rampant with his buddies. When he was alone, he longed for his mother for no particular reason and felt lonesome. Sometimes, lost in fascination at the sight of the mother next door, he indulged in memories of his own mother whose whereabouts in Okinawa remained unknown.

When his father began to talk of remarrying, Saburo openly displayed his ugly feelings. "Dad, if you bring a wife home, I'm out of here."

Saburo's father tolerated the harsh words with a pained look in his eyes. Soon, talk of remarriage evaporated.

His father was a serious, stern man. However, in his pain, Saburo sometimes blamed him for being a failure as a father and driving his mother to run away with her lover. Through the typical growing pains of adolescence, however, Saburo slowly matured as a person. Eventually he began to realize that his father had put everything into raising him. He saw that his father had given his blood, sweat, and tears so that his son could graduate from Saipan Vocational School. Even now, his father sent him the monthly tuition and dormitory fees. Gratitude finally sprouted in Saburo's heart.

Saburo enjoyed the two years he lived in the dormitory. He was in good physical shape, and in addition, he trained in judo. He often got into fights and mischief. The students who were older than Saburo gave him dirty looks and sometimes picked fights with him, but the younger students affectionately called him "Saburo-san." His naturally sunny personality, muscular build, and manliness made him popular.

During his second year at the vocational school, Saburo returned to Tinian on vacation to see his father. "You know, this island could become a battleground," Saburo's father said quietly one day.

A foreboding thought crossed Saburo's mind: *Could this be the last time I see my father?* As he boarded the ship returning to Saipan, he looked back at his father, who stood on the pier. His eyes appeared moist.

"Good luck, Saburo. Don't you die, now," Saburo's father murmured softly. When Saburo nodded, his father's sunburned face, engraved with hardships, softened slightly. When their eyes met, Saburo's father turned away to gaze out across the sea—far off to the northwest where lay Okinawa.

June 11, 1944, 1:00 P.M. On this day, like many others, Saburo was working in the agricultural-training pineapple farm at the foot of Mount Tapotchau in southern Garapan. Suddenly, sirens in town began to shriek. "Air raid! Air raid! Air raid! Everyone, to the shelter!"

Saburo and his classmates threw down their gardening hoes and jumped into the foxhole at the edge of the banana field. Explosions filled the air continuously. A huge explosion erupted in the city of Garapan, and smoke rose in the sky. One after another, the dark forms of U.S. aircraft emerged and swooped down from the smoky skies. Like arrows, bombshells cut through the sky and pierced the ground. Clouds of dust erupted, and the earth shook to its core with a resonating roar. The harbor and the town were bombed. The military base, still under construction, went up in repeated explosions. Pillars of flame rose from the sugar refinery in Chalan Kanoa to the south of Garapan, as well. Large formations of the U.S. planes joined in the attack, one after another. They blew up the light rail track that ran along the coast and a coastal gun-emplacement.

As the assault continued, Saburo and his classmates tried to burrow deeper into the ground, their bodies intertwined and folded over one other; their fingers plugging their ears and covering their eyes. Otherwise the explosion of the bombs and bullets landing closest to them could cause their eyeballs to fall out and their eardrums to burst.

The shelling didn't stop, but continued through a second, third, and fourth wave of planes. The antiaircraft and high-angle guns of the garrison were aimed at the attacking aircraft, but still the U.S. planes flew about freely. Saburo lifted his head. Japanese airplanes, with the red sun painted on their sides, flew toward the U.S. aircraft formation, but they were far too few in number. Once hit, they spouted fire and dropped into the ocean.

U.S. fighter planes came in low over a nearby army garrison location, raking the ground with gunfire. The sky was darkened by approaching aircraft spouting fire from the muzzles of the guns on the front edges of their wings. Saburo pulled his head close to his body and curled up as small as he could. Machine guns mowed down the banana grove. Saburo heard his classmates scream. A cloud of sand buried the foxhole.

The severe gunfire continued until sunset, pounding the entire island. In the aftermath, when the U.S. forces had finally left, a glow hung over the entire sky. "The school's burning!" shouted Saburo's classmate Isamu Sakiyama as he crawled out of the foxhole.

Flames enveloped the Saipan Vocational School building; the dormitory had already burned to the ground, and a gray pillar of smoke rose to the sky. Flames could be seen all over the city of Garapan. Saburo stood in the shadow of the banana grove and looked vacantly toward the city, the harbor, and the ocean, where ships were on fire.

It's here. . . . The inevitable had happened.

"Arakaki, do you think Tinian was hit, too?" darkness clouded Isamu Sakiyama's eyes as he spoke. He, too, had family in Tinian.

Saburo thought of his father. *Is he safe?* He recalled the expression on his father's face when he had speculated that the island could become a battleground. His eyes had seemed sad when he spoke those words. Perhaps it was because he had resigned himself to his unavoidable fate.

"Do you think the enemy will come to the island?" Skinny Sakiyama looked at Saburo with fear. Saburo could not shake his own inner dread. *I have to get rid of this fear,* he thought.

"If they're going to come, bring them on! If America attacks, we'll beat them to the ground! Yeah, let's fight them! Fight to the end!" As if building himself up to it, Saburo shook his clenched fists. Sakiyama did not respond; he was looking silently toward the ocean in the west. Black clouds billowed in the slowly darkening sky.

"Hey, you guys, come on! Gather around!" the head instructor called out. When the students had gathered, he announced, "This is a message from the principal. Students, return to your own homes and families. From now on, you will act in cooperation with your families. If you are a student who is not from this island, you will have to act on your own accord. You're dismissed."

The head instructor hastily made his exit. Most of the students started toward their homes. Did they have a home left? They all worried about their families.

"Act on your own accord?" *What did this mean?* Saburo had no where to go. His classmates Isamu Sakiyama and Yoshio Inami were in the same situation.

The city continued to burn. To Saburo, the horrible scene of the fiery night skies foreshadowed a coming major disaster. There were twenty-five thousand civilian Japanese and thirty-two hundred Chamorro and Kanaka civilian islanders living on Saipan. If Saipan became a battleground, these individuals would be entangled in the warfare.

In the darkness, flocks of families with children attempted their escape in a long line up Mount Tapotchau. Saburo and his two buddies moved to a cave at the foot of the mountain and spent the night there.

On that same day, aircraft based on carriers from the Fifty-eighth U.S. Navy Task Force attacked Aslito Airbase at the northern end of Saipan and destroyed 150 Japanese planes trapped on the ground. Twelve Japanese aircraft that intercepted the attack wave were shot down. U.S. forces also opened fire in a major attack on Tinian, Rota, and Guam. They succeeded in taking command of the air.

The U.S. forces had begun a full-scale military conquest of Saipan.

On the following day, June 12, U.S. forces returned before daybreak in full force to attack Saipan once more. The gunfire and bombing was intense. Few Japanese planes countered the U.S. forces. The exchange of gunfire in the air had already died down. For the troops in the Japanese reinforcement units who had barely landed, finding shelter in the natural surroundings was all they could manage to do. The weapons that had been unloaded were still stashed away. Machinery parts and ammunition were also stockpiled in large dumps, but these were destroyed in the gunfire.

Long after the U.S. forces had flown off, explosions continued from burning ammunition dumps.

Barely escaping disaster in the cave at the foot of the mountain, Saburo and his two buddies were forced to search for food on foot under the cover of night. The air in the fields and in the city was thick with the foul stench of gunpowder and burning human and animal flesh.

On June 13, just after 4:00 A.M., air raid sirens began to shriek once more. Some 250 U.S. planes stormed the Japanese bases and harbor facilities yet again, thoroughly destroying them.

Out at sea to the west at daybreak, the dark forms of countless warships filled the horizon.

"They've come!" Saburo shouted, pointing to the sea. Sakiyama timidly raised his head to peek out from the foxhole and looked out toward the sea. He swallowed hard, and his eyes filled with fear.

"The American forces . . ." Even Yoshio Inami, who was normally tough, was at a loss for words.

They had never, ever, seen so many warships. Saburo shuddered. *You must not be taken over by fear, he told himself.* Instead, he concentrated on stirring up feelings of hostility towards the Americans. "If you're going to come, come on! I'll kill ten of you by myself!" Fearlessness had been pounded into Saburo's head by the commissioned officer assigned to army training. "When the enemy disembarks, kill ten of them by yourself," the officer had said.

A little after 9:00 A.M., a row of destroyers appeared at the front. Far offshore in the distance Saburo and his friends could see large vessels that looked like a line of battleships and cruisers. He watched as each warship fired all of its guns in unison. They were stunned.

Shells flew through the air shrieking. Terrifying explosions shook the ground all around them. As Saburo fell prostrate, he saw a body blown into the air in front of him, along with earth and sand. Several times, he was buried in earth as bombs exploded nearby. The rumbling of the ground shook his internal organs. Paralyzed with terror, he found himself unable to move.

The terrifying storm of iron launched from the huge guns of the battleships swept over the entire island until the end of the day. The Japanese forces positioned on the shore were annihilated. The next day, the naval bombardment continued as well with the addition of attacks from the sky by aircraft. People whose shelters were directly hit were mowed down like ants as they ran about in terror trying to escape.

Suddenly several Japanese soldiers appeared at the cave where Saburo and his buddies were hiding. "Let us in!" The cave was small, and seeing that they all couldn't fit, the soldiers began to bark, "Noncombatants, get out! Out! Get out!"

With no other choice, Saburo and his buddies left the cave. Dropping to the ground at the shriek of flying shells and then running from exploding bombs, they searched for another natural shelter. In the shade of a grove of South Sea pines, they finally discovered another cave. They had managed to escape with their lives.

As the sun set, the shelling slowly died down, and the three boys stepped out of the cave to search for water and food. Besides having empty stomachs, they were terribly thirsty. There are no rivers in Saipan, and water was scarce. Private homes had tanks to collect rainwater, and Saburo and his two buddies went in search of such tanks. However, most of the concrete water tanks had been completely demolished in the bombing. All the teenagers could do was to moisten their throats with drops of muddy water from the bottom of what was left of the water tanks.

They were returning to their shelter at dusk when Yoshio Inami, who was in the lead, screamed and leaped back. A soldier's corpse lay on the ground. His internal organs were spilling out of his body. He had probably been hit by a shell from the naval bombardment.

"Hey, look over there." Isamu Sakiyama timidly pointed. Saburo cautiously followed his gaze. The cave from which the soldiers had chased them had received a direct hit and had collapsed. There also, dead bodies lay about. Goose bumps rose on Saburo's skin, and he was paralyzed by terror. His knees knocked together. *We could have been dead ourselves. . . . Death . . . this is what war is all about.*

Voiceless, the three boys looked at each other, and then, jolted by the horror of death, they took off running.

Chapter 4

Baptism of Fire

Pastor Arakaki stepped off the plane at Saipan International Airport on the southern tip of the island. The airport sits on the ruins of wartime Aslito Airbase. He blinked in the bright tropical sunlight, his deep emotions carefully locked within.

The island of Tinian was visible just to the south beyond a narrow, three-mile- (five-kilometer)-long strait. Tinian was where Pastor Arakaki spent ten years of his childhood with his father. His father, he recalled, had been trapped in the firestorm of battle those long years ago, and his body had never been found.

The group headed by car toward the city of Garapan. The road ran along the shore to the north. From Chalan Kanoa to Olei and Susupe, white-sand beaches lay to the left beside groves of coconut trees. On the right side of the road, beyond a grove of trees, was a monument in the shape of a cross, topped with an iron soldier's helmet. "That's a monument memorializing the landing of the U.S. forces," the driver explained.

The flame trees on the roadside were a bright vermilion.

"Let's stop and get out for a while." Pastor Arakaki got out and walked toward the white-sand beach. Miike joined him; the cameraman followed. Japanese tourists were enjoying the marine resort. Young windsurfers slid along the emerald green sea.

At the edge of the sea sat an abandoned tank, its brown, rusted turret exposed to the waves. On the beach, tank remains, relics of the war, lay where they had been tossed about in the salty breeze. Pastor Arakaki looked

31

out over the sea and said softly, "Landing craft covered this ocean . . . like raging waves."

* * * * *

On the morning of June 15, U.S. soldiers and marines headed toward Saipan's northwest shores and began to disembark after naval bombardments had pounded the Japanese position on the shore. The first wave of the landing unit included amphibious tanks and a flock of other landing craft; eight thousand marines stormed the entire shore from Olei to Chalan Kanoa south of Garapan.

The Japanese defensive positions had held their fire to this point, but now all the surviving machine guns in the shore positions unleashed a firestorm. However, the landing craft continued advancing, one after another, toward the shore in giant waves. The amphibious landing tank in the lead reached the shore, and the marines began hitting the beach.

From a cave in the mountains of southern Garapan, Saburo Arakaki watched the terrible, frightening battle expanding over the entire beach. Smashed into pieces by the naval bombardment, the gun positions of the Japanese force were buried in dirt and smoke and silenced. Near the shore, a desperate, hand-to-hand death struggle unfolded. From somewhere a cry arose, "The garrison from Olei is being finished off!"

Unable to stand the situation any longer, Saburo stood up. "Sakiyama, Inami, I'm going to join up with the army!" He looked at Yoshio Inami and Isamu Sakiyama, the buddies with whom he had stayed until then. "I'm going!"

The light shining in Saburo's eyes showed his determination. His two friends looked at him with resolute expressions and nodded in agreement. The three youths left the cave and headed toward the garrison near the farm's training grounds. When Grumman fighter craft approached in the sky above, they hid in the shadow of brush and shrubs. They learned to determine how far away a targeted area was by listening to the screaming of shells flying through the air. They ran between explosions, then threw themselves flat on the ground when airplanes flew overhead—over and over again until they finally arrived at the garrison. There, soldiers ran about in a frenzy.

"Let us help out!"

A lance corporal wearing eyeglasses consented. "Fine. How many of you are there?" Saburo turned around to find that only Inami remained with him; Sakiyama had vanished. He had been with them when they were hiding in the shrubbery. Where had he gone?

"All right! Help us haul food to the Olei garrison," the lance corporal said.

Following the corporal's order, Saburo and Inami, along with three soldiers, picked up billy clubs and advanced under a shower of bullets. One soldier fell to the ground, his side gouged out by a fragment of a shell that exploded at close range. It was too risky to approach the area around Olei because of the severe fighting. While they looked for a chance to move on, the injured soldier breathed his last.

Reluctantly, the men retreated to the garrison at Garapan. Several dozen injured soldiers lay on the ground after having been dragged in from the battle. Saburo and Inami were given a bag of crackers, but before they even had a chance to fill their starved stomachs, they were ordered to help transport the wounded soldiers.

American tanks were landing on the beach at Olei and Chalan Kanoa. The Japanese army continued to wage a desperate struggle. American enemy forces surrounded a company of the Japanese antiaircraft regiment that no longer had firepower and charged at them. When the sun had set and the Grumman aircraft circling overhead had withdrawn, a heavy artillery position that had been firing from a hidden position in the valley at the foot of Mount Tapotchau ceased firing altogether. A 150 mm howitzer continued to expend its shells on the twenty thousand U.S. marines that had established a beachhead along the entire shoreline.

That night, the Japanese carried out a desperate, death-defying night raid on the U.S. marine invasion force along the beach. However, the U.S. troops quickly discovered the Japanese plan to attack under the cover of night and fired brightly burning flare bombs that illuminated the *shirotatsuki,* or white headbands, of the night attack corps closing in upon the U.S.

forces. Gunfire spouted from the machine guns positioned by the U.S. military who had been awaiting their arrival. Japanese tank corps charged the American enemy, along with the shock troops. Tracers from the cross-fire entangled in the air, and the entire beachfront became a sea of fire. At the receiving end of the stubborn retaliation from the U.S. troops, thirty Japanese tanks from the night attack corps were destroyed. The Japanese troops finally retreated, leaving behind seven hundred casualties.

The night raid was repeated the following night, but again the night attack corps failed to recapture lost territory. It succeeded only in raising a mountain of corpses.

With reinforcements to the landing corps and bomb support from sea and sky, the U.S. troops advanced inland, with tanks in the lead. The marine division that had disembarked over the entire Chalan Kanoa area spread out over the hilltop of Fina Susu, to the south as well as to Aslito Airbase. From the Olei beach position, a marine division marched towards Mount Tapotchau and the city of Garapan. Hiding in foxholes, the Japanese garrison carried out a desperate struggle. Fierce battles broke out along the way.

One after another, the Japanese defense positions were annihilated before the overwhelming gunfire from the U.S. troops. The remaining guards were forced to retreat toward Mount Tapotchau, even while continuing to resist the advancing U.S. troops.

Saburo gasped for breath as he climbed through the jungle halfway up Mount Tapotchau with a wounded officer on his back. He parted brush as he went, struggling through the thick tropical growth along a path made by fleeing refugees. Sweat trickled from his face, and his throat was parched. His arms and legs were stained with blood from snagging his skin on thorns and the sharp edges of rock.

Shells showered onto the mountainside as well. Stepping out onto the roadside and carelessly exposing himself, Saburo was met with a round of persistent machine gunfire from Grumman aircraft patrolling overhead.

Here and there lay the corpses of refugees, and a nauseating stench wafted through the air. Somewhere along the way, Saburo had become separated from Yoshio Inami.

The peak of Mount Tapotchau rose 1,550 feet (473 meters) above sea level. Saburo began to move from the southern side of the mountain toward the east. Ascending and descending valley after valley, he headed even farther north past the hills along the eastern coast. His goal was to reach the field hospital at Donnay on the northeast side at the base of Mount Tapotchau. Also located there was the island's only water source.

"Arakaki. Let me down for a bit." Master Sergeant Aoki spoke between painful breaths. Saburo unloaded the sergeant's heavy frame at the foot of a tree. Leaning against the trunk of the tree, the sergeant frantically gasped for air. A machine gun bullet had passed through his thigh, and blood seeped through the bandage covering the wound.

Earlier, Saburo and the group he was with had faced severe gunfire as they headed from southern Garapan to the front line to rescue wounded soldiers. They took shelter in the nearest foxhole but were unable to move any farther. Master Sergeant Aoki had been shot down and stranded about ten to twenty meters ahead. He waved his hand for help, but none of the soldiers had the nerve to leave the foxhole. Shells shrieked overhead, grazing the tops of heads that peeked out of the foxhole.

He'll be killed for sure if he's left out there! Saburo leaped out of the foxhole. He rushed to the sergeant, who was unable to walk, and dragged him back into the foxhole. As the shelling died down, the men retreated to save their lives. Saburo accompanied them, carrying the sergeant on his back.

Once emergency measures had been taken to stop the sergeant's bleeding, he asked Saburo in a weak voice, "What unit are you from?" Like the soldiers, Saburo was wearing camouflage khaki shirt and pants, and his legs were wrapped in leggings.

"Me?" Saburo answered. "I'm a student at the Saipan Vocational School."

"Oh. Well, thank you," the sergeant said gratefully. "I'm Aoki, originally from Gifu Prefecture." He was perhaps twenty-seven or twenty-eight. The sergeant blinked; his eyes showed no trace of cockiness.

A young general ordered Saburo to carry Sergeant Aoki to the field hospital at Donnay.

Saburo had now been carrying the sergeant on his back through the mountain for three days and two nights. They had had no food or water. When night fell, Saburo descended to the base of the mountain to search for sweet potato fields. He dug up some sweet potatoes and gathered a bit of muddy water into his canteen from the bottom of demolished water tanks. Sometimes they soothed their thirst with sugarcane.

The field hospital at Donnay was located in a gulch in the shade of a grove of South Sea pines. The temporary clinic was completely filled with wounded soldiers. After receiving only the simplest treatment, Sergeant Aoki was laid down in a natural shelter nearby. Three thousand wounded men lay around him on the grass and on rocks, all begging for water. "Please, I'm thirsty, give me water. Give me water."

Dodging shells, Saburo made trip after trip to the water source.

Saburo learned from soldiers who arrived at Donnay that his friend Yoshio Inami had been shot in the head by a machine gun in an aircraft attack and had died instantly. *Inami . . . dead!* It was a shock. Saburo was seized with sorrow, but no tears flowed. He had already seen too much death. It seemed that death lurked nearby for him as well.

There were countless refugees in the surrounding jungle with no place to go. From deep within the brush came the cries of infants and voices like eerie screams. Mothers whose breasts had stopped giving milk watched their babies die, and they began to go crazy. The women roamed through the jungle, their kimonos hanging open.

The sound of gunfire was incessant.

"Our troops have abandoned Aslito Airbase."

"The enemy has entered Garapan."

Moment by moment, urgent battle reports came in. Soldiers who fought from the natural gulch where they were holed up were torched or killed with hand grenades. The rumor was that the majority of the soldiers who had been driven out of the trenches with gas bombs had refused to surrender and were then shot to death.

"Avoid the disgrace of being captured alive and the shame of dying." This was the battlefront order for Japanese soldiers, who were forbidden to surrender. Saburo, too, had recited this order during his military training.

In the face of overwhelming firepower by the U.S. troops, the Japanese garrison was being destroyed left and right; no alternative was left but certain defeat. U.S. troops were also advancing from the south toward Lau Lau Bay to the east. At this rate, how long could the resistance from Mount Tapotchau possibly hold out?

"No doubt a combined fleet will back us up."

"The plan is to counterattack and wipe out the enemy."

Such stories filtered through the circle of soldiers.

It's got to be true. Saburo believed it with all his might. *There's no way our unrivaled combined fleet would ever just hand over Saipan to the enemy.*

"Sergeant, it looks like we need to hold out just a little longer, doesn't it? Surely the combined fleet is coming to save us. . . ."

Aoki didn't reply but gazed upward with clouded eyes at the ceiling of the cave.

On June 17, two days after the U.S. troops had landed, the Imperial Headquarters executed plans for reinforcing Saipan. The combined fleet stood ready to destroy U.S. troops in a decisive battle. Strategy "A" was put into operation. Around a nucleus of 9 aircraft carriers, 7 battleships, 73 naval vessels, and 439 ship-borne aircraft, the Japanese First Mobile Fleet advanced eastward in Philippine waters. It was a huge battle formation that highlighted the strength of the combined fleet.

U.S. Task Force Fifty-eight had already anticipated that the combined fleet would come out. The reconnaissance planes of the Japanese First Mobile Fleet soon sighted the U.S. Task Group advancing to the west of Saipan. The Japanese fleet planned to use the long cruising range of its carrier-based planes to its advantage. The initial attack strategy was to launch an attack beyond the range of the U.S. carrier-based aircraft. On the morning of June 19, the Japanese First Mobile Fleet launched an attack force that numbered 246 planes, a massive force that outnumbered the planes used to attack Pearl Harbor.

U.S. Task Force Fifty-eight had not yet located the Japanese fleet. However, the Americans quickly detected the Japanese attack by radar, and 450 fighter planes awaited the Japanese in the sky. The Japanese planes were attacked by an overwhelming force. In the sky above the task force, they were destroyed one after another by newly developed antiaircraft shells using VT fuse technology that allowed shells to explode near the aircraft's fuselage to down the targeted plane. The devastation was so massive that the Americans later named it the Great Turkey Shoot of the Marianas. The attack mounted by the second wave of 82 planes could be described only as pitiful and yielded no more than a few near misses.

On the first day of the attack, the Japanese First Mobile Fleet lost 193 planes and had 2 aircraft carriers sunk by submarines. In exchange, the losses by the U.S. forces were minor: 17 planes shot down and 5 ships, including battleships, sunk.

The following day, on the twentieth, the U.S. Task Force pursued the Japanese fleet. It attacked with 216 aircraft, sinking 1 Japanese aircraft carrier and showering 4 others with direct hits. The Japanese First Mobile Fleet launched 10 torpedo planes, but the attack failed, and most of them were lost. In the battles of those two days, the Japanese forces lost 395 planes.

The Battle of the Marianas eventually led to the massive unilateral defeat of the Japanese fleet. The Japanese lost command of both the sea and the air to the U.S. forces and no longer had the military strength to recapture Saipan. On June 24, at the General Headquarters in Tokyo, the inevitable decision was made to terminate the plan to reinforce Saipan and to surrender the island.

However, this decision was not disclosed to Saipan until the very end.

Unaware that they had been abandoned, the military and civilians in Saipan continued to defend their island, all the while fervently awaiting their rescue. Among them was Saburo Arakaki.

Chapter 5

Fleeing North

At a beachside hotel in Garapan, Pastor Arakaki changed out of his traveling clothes. Dressed lightly, he quickly slipped on a pair of sneakers and headed outdoors. He gazed up at the summit of Mount Tapotchau, three miles (five kilometers) to the northeast.

Looking at Arakaki, Miike began to see beyond the figure of a respected pastor to the young Saburo Arakaki who, as a student at the Saipan Vocation School, had become caught up in the war that had come to the island.

On that very mountain and in the hills that continued to the north slept thousands—no, tens of thousands—of Japanese and Americans alike who had lost their lives in battle.

* * * * *

Mount Tapotchau was a natural stronghold. The U.S. forces, intent on capturing the summit, met dogged resistance from the Japanese forces, and the ensuing fierce battle resulted in extensive bloodshed. The U.S. forces fought a particularly brutal battle in the northeast valley, where so many lives were lost it was called the Valley of Death.

However, the courageous attempt by the Japanese to defend the summit to the death didn't last long in the face of overwhelming U.S. firepower. The Americans advanced from the eastern beaches toward the summit, and on June 26, they captured the summit at last.

Peril advanced toward the field hospital at Donnay, as well. Shells exploded all around, and the number of casualties multiplied. The hospital chief issued a final command: "Those of you who can fight, fight. Those who are wounded, make your way to the north. Those of you who are unable to move, prepare for death."

A stir arose among the wounded soldiers. To Saburo's horror, right before his eyes, hand grenades were handed out to the seriously wounded to be used by those who chose an honorable death instead of surrender.

The wounded sang the war chorus, "Umi Yukuba," in unison. Then those who were still able to move began to crawl toward the jungle brush. Soon Saburo heard a voice cry out, "Mother!" and then a hand grenade exploded with a terrifying roar. The sound of exploding hand grenades continued. And then, a single gunshot. Saburo would later learn that the hospital chief, feeling responsible for the loss of lives, had committed suicide as well.

With tanks in the lead, the U.S. forces advanced. The field hospital was surrounded on three sides. The attack was carried on into the night, until, with hardly any ability left to fight, the soldiers at the field hospital were nearly completely annihilated.

Saburo had not even a handgun with which to fight. Helping the injured Sergeant Aoki, Saburo took refuge on a craggy cliff in the jungle a short distance from Donnay. However, they desperately needed to escape or they would face certain death. The sergeant had recovered somewhat from his wounds, so they crawled up the mountain slope, emerging on a ridge on Telegraph Mountain, so named for the wireless radio station situated there. Combined Japanese naval and army headquarters had been set up in a cave on the west side of the mountain.

The Americans continued to fire flare bombs, even after nightfall, shelling the island from sea and sky. Saburo and Sergeant Aoki fled north amid a barrage of exploding shells that illuminated the night like day. Crouching in the shadow of boulders and in craters left by bombs, hiding and then running again, they fled north—always north. The southern half of the island had already been captured. Saipan is an island only twelve and a half miles long (twenty kilometers), north to south. Fleeing to the north, one eventually comes to the end of the island, with nowhere to go. But even though they knew they were headed toward a place of no escape, the refugees continued fleeing north. The only remaining glimmer of hope was the belief that the Japanese Combined Fleet would come to their rescue. The thirsty and hungry snatched up the belongings of the dead and dying; fights broke out over water canteens. The corpses of refugees and soldiers became noticeably more numerous the farther north Saburo and Sergeant Aoki went.

Japan would never give us up to be killed. There's no way the Divine Nation of Japan can lose. Surely our allies will save us. Until then, we must keep going! On the brink of losing heart, Saburo prodded himself forward.

The sun set, and at some point the bombing subsided. On the jungle path, beaten down by fleeing feet, Saburo staggered forward, the sergeant leaning on his shoulder.

"I'm finished. Just leave me here." Time and again, the sergeant collapsed, out of breath. His unshaven face was gaunt, and his eyes pained.

"Aoki-san, you must pull yourself together or you'll die by the roadside," Saburo urged. After letting the sergeant catch his breath, Saburo would start walking again, one of the sergeant's arms draped around his shoulder. There wasn't even a drop of water left in the canteen. Saburo himself was suffering from hunger and thirst, and he was exhausted.

In the shadow of a boulder, Saburo finally lay down on the ground and looked up at the sky. All the stars in the sky were aglow.

"It's so quiet, isn't it?" Sergeant Aoki whispered.

In the deathly silence between bouts of shelling, they watched the twinkling of the stars, and the reality of an island ravaged by battle fires seemed strangely unreal. *I'm alive still, somehow,* Saburo thought. He recalled his father's parting words in Tinian—*"Don't you die, now."* Has *the enemy landed on Tinian, too? Is my father still alive?* For a fleeting moment, the image of his mother passed through his mind. *I wonder how she is these days?*

Whether she was happy or sad, his mother's eyes had always been dark and lustrous. He could see them now, although he had no idea where she might be.

Those childhood days when the whole family had played together at the beach in Okinawa—Saburo, Father, Mother, his brother and sisters. The tiny bright blue fish in the tidal pools in the coral reef. The white shells they had collected together. Although poverty-stricken, they had had a peaceful life. All of that was now a dream of a long ago, faraway place. Before he knew it, Saburo had fallen asleep.

In the half-light just before dawn, he heard voices. The sudden sound awakened him. *Americans?* He stiffened for a moment, but then he heard the sounds of Japanese. Three soldiers passed by.

"Sirs, do you know of any food anywhere?" Saburo asked spontaneously.

Learning that Saburo, a vocational school student, was transporting a wounded officer, they answered, "There's a warehouse at Matansa with provisions. Try going there."

The village of Matansa is situated on a flat piece of land facing the sea on the northwest side of the island. Urging Sergeant Aoki along, Saburo descended the mountain slopes.

A road ran along the shore from the town of Garapan to the northern end of the island. All along that road lay corpses, giving off a rotten stench. The dark forms of military stragglers and civilians crept along in the dim light with unsteady footsteps, like those of sleepwalkers, all headed north.

Saburo and the sergeant also followed the road north, and in the shadow of a grove of South Sea pines near the mountainside, they found the naval provisions warehouse, but it had been demolished in the shelling. Hardly a trace of the building remained. The stench of rotting food wafted through the air, along with the foul odor of the dead soldiers lying strewn every which way. Digging his way through the rubble, his nose as sharp as that of a starving, homeless dog, Saburo found some buried food.

"It's hardtack, Sergeant Aoki! And look what else I've found! Canned red-bean rice! Canned crab!"

"Thank goodness!"

The two stuffed their shoulder bags and pockets with all the canned goods they could carry. A meager amount of muddy water had collected at the bottom of the demolished water tank. They scooped it out into a canteen.

"Arakaki, let's get out of here. It's dangerous here. The bombing is going to start up," the sergeant insisted. They dove into the jungle and began to crawl up the mountain slope. Behind them rose the sounds of exploding bombs. Shells screamed overhead.

"Sergeant, over here!" Saburo rolled into a cave, the sergeant close behind.

After that they could only leave their fate to the heavens. As shells exploded all around, Saburo devoured the food in his hands, hardly stopping to catch his breath.

For three days, they hid in that tiny cave. The massive air raids and continued bombing made it impossible to leave. They ate the canned goods and moistened their throats with the muddy water. They rested their exhausted bodies. Sergeant Aoki seemed to regain some strength.

"If I had a cane, I could walk on my own," he smiled weakly for the first time. The bombing continued. And now, interspersed with the sound of explosions, they could hear in the distance the sharp crack of small arms fire, like the pop of roasting beans. And mixed in with the sharp popping was the jarring rumble of heavy machine guns. The sergeant's eyes darkened.

"This isn't good. The enemy is coming." The American assault troops were advancing—even Saburo understood this.

"What should we do, Aoki-san?"

"When it gets dark, let's get out of here."

"Where will we go?"

"North. We can only go north."

"To Banadero? There's nowhere to go after that."

The sergeant swallowed hard.

Banadero was the island's northernmost point. If one arrived there, only the sea remained beyond that. Unable to retreat or advance from there, they would face certain death.

"But if we stay here, we'll only be shot to death."

"That's right."

"Arakaki, if it has come to this, let's just try to survive as long as we can."

"Yes, sir."

The two looked at each other with grave eyes and nodded. Then the sergeant turned away and murmured, "The question is . . . just how many more days we will be able to survive."

The sun set, and even though the sound of the guns on land died down, shells flew without reprieve from the warships anchored offshore. Flare bombs continued to explode, leaving no chance for the island to be enveloped in the darkness of night. In the few seconds between flare bombs, Saburo and the sergeant left the cave. Weaving between trees in the jungle, they headed north on the slopes. Under the hail of exploding bombs, they simply fled in desperation.

I don't want to die like this, in the bombing. Just get me away from the sound of the shelling, Saburo thought.

They heard, somewhere deep in the jungle, the chilling scream of a woman. Children were crying out for help. With Sergeant Aoki's physical condition in mind, Saburo plowed forward in the direction of Banadero, all the while knowing that they headed straight for the land of death.

Chapter 6

Rainbow Over Hell

In a station wagon generously loaned to the group by an American dentist, Pastor Arakaki, Miike, and the TV crew headed toward the northern end of the island from Garapan, along the Marpi Road that runs northward along the western shore of the island. The region, from Matansa to the foot of northernmost Mount Marpi (817 feet or 249 meters above sea level) and stretching out to Banadero, was the site of the banzai charge, where the Japanese troops made their final attack against the Americans, sacrificing their lives for the honor of the motherland.

Today, peace monuments and memorials for the dead stand all over this area. Tourists aim their cameras at the wreckage of Japanese cannons and tanks standing back to back.

The jagged cliffs of northern Mount Marpi are collectively called Suicide Cliff. Cornered there, Japanese women threw themselves to their deaths on the rocky terrain 787 feet (240 meters) below. Countless soldiers and civilians plunged into the ocean from the lower cliffs along the coast also. Today, this area is named Banzai Cliff. A chalky memorial to the dead, the Tower of the Pacific Ocean, stands there overlooking the sea. This was the far end of the island, the place where life came to an end. Beyond, there is only the ocean.

Pastor Arakaki paused to gaze out over the open sea. At his side, Miike was silent. Turning, the pastor looked up at the cliffs of Mount Marpi. As never before, his gaze was stony. Forty-three years earlier, eighteen-year-old Saburo had stood at the precipice of those same cliffs.

* * * * *

udy with gunpowder smoke. A flock of black U.S. war-
he island, as though they did not intend to let a single
. Those the enemy had killed covered the ground. The
warships spouted gunfire continuously, and shells flew screaming through
the air, mercilessly slaughtering those who hid themselves in the shadows
of boulders and in the jungle.

Saburo had come to Mount Marpi, climbing the mountain slopes from
Matansa. Now with nowhere else to flee, he stood on the edge of the jagged
cliffs with Sergeant Aoki. Below lay the flat stretch of ground at Banadero,
and they could see that the runway, which had been under construction for
the naval base, had been demolished in the bombing. Several hundred feet
to the north, cliffs plunged into the ocean from Adan's green-shrubbed terrain. Marpi Point, jutting slightly to the northwest, was the farthest point
of Saipan's northern tip.

Fleeing soldiers and civilians pressed themselves into any shelter they
could find; the shadow of even the smallest boulder was better than no
shelter at all. Enemy planes circled overhead like bloodthirsty bald eagles,
and in the jungle, dead bodies lay scattered about. Human flesh clung to
trees and rocks.

From the south, rifle shots rang out, intermingled with the roar of
bombs. Saburo knew that moment by moment the enemy was closing in
around them.

Every so often, from all directions in the jungle came the sound of a
hand grenade exploding. Another person had decided to make the ultimate
sacrifice.

"Kill me, please!"

"Sir, kill me!"

They could hear the cries of women. Then grotesque shrieks. Screams.
The raging groans of men. Children crying. Suddenly, a young girl burst
out of the jungle. She ran, disheveled hair flying, to the edge of the cliff and
flung herself into the air. Other women followed, throwing themselves off
the cliff. Voicelessly, as if being sucked into hell, they fell.

This *was* hell.

It was the beginning of July. Almost twenty days had passed since the American forces had landed. *It's amazing that we've come this far; that I've managed to help Sergeant Aoki survive; that we've retreated all the way,* thought Saburo. However, now he knew that there was nowhere else they could flee. Death was closing in. Sergeant Aoki stretched out near the top of the cliff. Nearby, Saburo lay in the shelter of a boulder and quietly watched the ocean to the north.

I'm going to die here. He resigned himself to his fate.

As if to mock the now-submissive Japanese forces, U.S. gunboats navigated the water slowly, firing from a few hundred feet offshore. The rhythmic, ear-splitting explosions drove Saburo to the brink of insanity, dulling his sense of judgment. *Ahhh . . . how simple it would be if I were just hit directly. I don't care anymore if I die.* Utterly overcome with despair, Saburo felt the strength drain from his body and mind. *When will it be? When will I finally be hit?*

With nothing left to do, Saburo stared out at the ocean.

Suddenly, to the far left in his field of vision, something blue began to move. Fifty feet away, a girl in a blue shirt got up from the small crevice in which she had been lying. The young girl's hair was cut into a bob; she was perhaps ten years old. As if she were dreaming, the girl stood up with a gentle, delicate motion.

"Lie down!" Saburo shouted at her, forgetting himself completely. "That's dangerous!" She stood in a crevice near the edge of the cliff. Even if she weren't directly hit, a bomb blast could blow her over the edge.

The girl turned slowly. He saw a white face erased of fear, an absent look in her dark, unblinking eyes. He had seen a face like that somewhere before. . . .

"Lie down! Lie down!" Saburo waved his arms and shouted. Did she hear him? Suddenly, a pure smile surfaced in her white face.

Saburo swallowed hard.

The young girl held up both hands, and made a gentle gesture, like dancing. At that moment, a roar—then a tremendous explosion and flashing lights—detonated all at once. Saburo lost consciousness. Pounded by the blast, he lay sprawled on the rocky ground. At some point, consciousness returned, and he realized that by some good fortune he was not wounded. *That little girl . . . what happened to her?* He looked toward the crevice.

There had been a direct hit on the spot where she had been standing. Nearby lay the twisted bodies of two soldiers, limbs torn off, but otherwise there was nothing. No trace of the little girl in the blue shirt; she had been scattered to the four winds. In an instant, a child's life had been snuffed out.

Saburo was overcome more by bewilderment than by fear. There was a violent ringing in his ears. He could hear nothing, as if he had been flung out into empty space. Still in a state of foggy consciousness, he found himself unable to move, and he looked blankly toward the open sea. The surrounding scene looked faded in color—gray even. Even the glaring flashes from the large guns on the warships didn't catch his attention. It all looked like a scene from another world. Beyond that horizon was Japan. In Okinawa was Mother. *I want to go to Japan. Home to Okinawa.* But home was so far away, too far away; it was like a dream.

Saburo simply stared at the ocean. A pale light radiated from the water not too far offshore. Was it an illusion? The yellow radiance took on a reddish tinge on one side, then combined with green, blue, and purple, it rose from the surface of the sea and climbed skyward.

What is it?

It became a rainbow, standing on the ocean at a perpendicular angle. Rising high above the surface of the sea, it finally melted into the sky.

Ahh, it's a rainbow!

Saburo's heart suddenly softened, and he was enraptured by the mysterious spectacle before his eyes. Without thinking he raised himself and slowly stood up. The rainbow fascinated him. It was moving, very gently, toward the shore.

It's coming this way! He watched in fascination.

It climbed the cliffs along the shore, ascended onto the land, and headed straight for him. Didn't anyone else notice this battlefield rainbow?

The rainbow passed over the Banadero jungle and kept coming— toward the precipice where Saburo stood.

With eyes wide and breath bated, he waited for it to reach him. As it approached, it grew, and when it had spread over the entire sky, Saburo found himself wrapped in its gentle light. Without a sound, showers from heaven rained down on him. Saburo looked up into the sky. The gentle drizzle was refreshing. A rainbow over hell. Heaven-sent rain. The rain bathed his face. Raindrops moistened his tongue. As he swallowed the precious drops of rain, a feeling of rejuvenation flooded his soul.

With the rain came a feeling of unsurpassed peace; like a man liberated from the terror of death, Saburo raised his hands to the heavens. *Thank you.*

Along with the drops of rain shed from the rainbow, something hot and salty filled his eyes.

"Watch out!"

Suddenly someone seized Saburo around the waist and slammed him to the ground. The sound of exploding shells filled the air. "Arakaki! What's wrong with you?" Sergeant Aoki looked at Saburo suspiciously.

"The rainbow . . ." Saburo murmured, a smile on his wet face. "Did you see it? The beautiful rainbow?"

Chapter 7

Banzai Attack

In order to film the region of the cape in its entirety, the crew turned the car toward Suicide Cliff. The clearing at the top of the cliff had been turned into a Peace Memorial Park. Atop a white pedestal three meters tall stood a cross and a statue of Kannon, the goddess of mercy.

Pastor Arakaki stood before the monument, eyes closed, and prayed for peace for the victims of the war. Miike stood at the edge of the cliff. The cliff rose so sharply from the sea—perpendicular almost—that if it hadn't been for the handrails, he would have felt weak in the knees. Miike had seen it many times—the U.S. military's documentary film clip in which a woman dressed in traditional Japanese work clothes flings her body into the air from this very cliff. And every time, it made his throat tighten.

All around stood countless wooden grave markers, erected there by memorial groups from Japan. Red hibiscus flowers swayed in the breeze that blew in from the sea. How many had looked out over the endless sea to the north, wishing to return to their motherland, Japan. To see loved ones— just once more before their lives were snatched away. Miike pressed his palms together and bowed his head, thinking of the souls of the war victims.

The sun tilted to the west, and the ocean began to glow a brilliant gold. A gentle shower, like a drizzle, passed through the area, dampening the ground without a sound.

Pastor Arakaki called out, "There's a rainbow out there, most likely."

"Yes. Most likely. Somewhere." Miike smiled. The battleground rainbow of which Pastor Arakaki had spoken threaded through his mind in a dazzling image. It rose up in seven brilliant colors from a sea filled with gunpowder smoke.

"That day seems like a dream," Pastor Arakaki said, referring to the morning of desperation and defeat, forty-three years earlier.

* * * * *

July 6. Morning dawned after a ghastly night that could only have been a nightmare. After a long interval of rainless weather, a sudden squall broke loose. The merciless bombing by the American forces continued. Worn to the breaking point, civilians in ever greater numbers gave up hope and flung themselves, one after another, from the cliff into the ocean. The bodies that fell on the rocks below floated about in the shallow water. Here and there on the beach, clothing and canteens had been discarded. From time to time, shredded photographs and bits of paper money were swept up in a bomb blast. In their last moments of life, people had discarded even their most precious possessions.

Along with Sergeant Aoki, Saburo descended Mount Marpi and hid in Banadero's jungle. Soldiers and civilians mingled together enveloped in an air of tension and despair. Saburo looked around to see if he could spot any students from the Saipan Vocational School, but he didn't see anyone he recognized.

Now everything was futile. Saburo unwound what little paper money he had kept wrapped in the handkerchief tied around his waist and threw it out. It was inevitable that the U.S. troops would launch an all-out attack from land and sea—perhaps even tomorrow. Anxiety and despair began to overwhelm Saburo.

When the sun set that evening, the shelling subsided. Soldiers began moving about even more frantically. The moon rose in the eastern sky. A military messenger came running. "There's to be a massive counterattack! Gather around!"

Voices began calling out. "It's a division command order! Gather around!"

In the moonlight, a commissioned officer began shouting at the several hundred soldiers who had gathered in the area surrounding Banadero Airport: "Today, both Navy Vice Admiral Nagumo and Army Lieutenant General Saito, at the combined headquarters at Hell Valley, made the decision to die an honorable death!"

A moan, like unspeakable bewilderment, rose from the crowd. A heavy air enveloped them.

The commanding officer was dead! *What are we to do?*

Instinctively, Saburo looked at Sergeant Aoki's face. The sergeant had sat down, his shoulders drooping and eyes closed.

"I give to all of you the final order of the commander in chief!"

In the dim moonlight, another commissioned officer unfolded a piece of paper in his hands and read in a loud voice: "Message to the imperial forces, Saipan. For over two weeks since the attack by the U.S. forces . . ."

The soldiers fell into a dead silence and a flock of eyes—some ferocious, some flinching, others dark with despair, and still others eyes glinting with rage—took in the words of the commanding officer with a frozen, death-like gaze.

". . . We have no battle supplies left, our munitions have been destroyed, our comrades are perishing one after another. . . . The U.S. forces have taken a small corner of Saipan, but the shelling and bombardment is severe. . . . Death is near."

There were some words Saburo didn't understand, but he understood that the Japanese forces had lost, and that they faced certain death.

". . . Whether we attack or hold out, we will die. When that time comes, we have the opportunity to show that we are true men of the Japanese empire. One more attack will be advanced on the U.S. forces, and a bulwark will be erected for the Pacific on Saipan with the bones that we bury and leave. According to battlefield ethics, 'I vow never to suffer the disgrace of being taken alive but will rise up with my entire being in courage and dignity, rejoicing in living according to the eternal principle of justice until the end.' "

Those militaristic words pierced Saburo's ears: "I vow never to suffer the disgrace of being taken alive." During military training at school, he had memorized and daily recited these words over and over again. Men and boys of Japan must never be taken as prisoners of war—it had been pounded into his brain. Now he faced the reality of this supreme order.

"I give you this command!" The commissioned officer raised his voice even further. "The Saipan garrison shall mount an attack on the American devils tomorrow, July 7, with each man killing ten Americans and fighting to an honorable death." The order was for a banzai charge against the American camp, with the desperate purpose of killing even one additional American until no Japanese was left to fight.

"Death for honor! Death for honor!" a great stir rose from among the soldiers.

"You are ordered to seek out the threatening enemy forces tomorrow, July 7, anytime after 15:30, and attack, advancing toward Chalan Kanoa to pulverize the American forces," the officer continued.

"Oh . . . Oh, no . . ." Heavy moans that could not be made into words shook the crowd.

Any hope of being saved had collapsed. Soldiers began to move about.

It has come—the final moment! Anxiety ran up his spine, and Saburo shuddered. *For the motherland, for the Divine Emperor! I'm going to give my life! Die a noble death! As a Japanese, I'll have a dignified end! I will never be taken prisoner!* Spurring himself on, Saburo roused his resolve.

"Sergeant Aoki, I'm going with you!" Saburo put his determination into words.

The sergeant nodded. "You've really taken care of me." With a weak smile, he thumped Saburo on the back.

Two surprise attack units were organized, made up not only of soldiers but also of civilians and volunteer supporters. Saburo was placed in the second unit. Those who did not have other weapons bound daggers to the end of sticks. Those who didn't even have sticks and daggers made spears out of raw branches.

It was July 7, *Tanabata,* the Festival of the Weaver Star, just past midnight, and the festival moon hung in midheaven. "Gather at Matansa and advance toward the enemy at Tanapag. Let's go!" the commissioned officer barked out the order, and the first attack unit of four hundred or so persons quietly began to advance toward Matansa on the western shore. The sense of death moved about like a breeze through the night. Everyone—those on the road along the shore and those on the road along the mountainside—

walked silently forward, exposed to the enemy, not even crouching low to the ground or hiding in the shadows.

Saburo strained his eyes to gaze after the soldiers whose backs faded away in the distance. In the dim moonlight, the flock of ghostly shadows, like something not of this world, vanished into the darkness where something dreadful was developing.

With a spear carved from wood in his hand, Saburo stood for some time. The moon disappeared in the western sky, and the area was shrouded in complete darkness. Suddenly, in the distance, the roar of a machine gun tore through the silence. At the same moment, the terrible scream of the banzai charge burst and swelled in the air. The wild, crazed death voices made Saburo's intestines churn and raised goose bumps on his skin. At the same time, blood charged through his veins. He was confused and felt paralyzed. Flashes of light pierced the darkness. Flare bombs burst in the sky, one after another. The sound of fierce shelling and bombardment, like the roar of the ocean, drowned out the screaming. Like the ebbing of the tides, the voices were swept away.

Saburo gritted his teeth and almost took off running. Sergeant Aoki took his hand and held him in position.

The second attack unit was put into motion, and both Saburo and Sergeant Aoki joined in at the tail end. Each of the three hundred or so members of the group was given a single rice ball cooked in salt water. Without savoring it, without feeling thankful, without feeling anything at all, Saburo devoured his portion.

Suddenly a flustered commissioned officer appeared on the scene, shouting loudly. "Everybody, listen up! A warship left Tokyo Bay today to save Saipan! Let's survive until that ship arrives! Live and fight! That's it!"

A sea of voices rose from the crowd. Some clasped each other's hands. No one questioned the officer's words. It hardly seemed like a false report.

"Aoki-san, let's go back to the jungle," Saburo urged.

Whatever it takes, we've got to go on living, he thought. Those who had resolved, just moments before, to die with honor for the motherland and the Divine Emperor now had to make a complete turnabout; now they had to determine to survive and continue fighting.

Saburo and the sergeant turned around and retreated into the jungle. They found a crevice in a boulder and hid there.

When morning dawned, the shelling concentrated on the area around Banadero. The American troops advanced to Mount Marpi as well, wiping out the Japanese troops. Those who ran about in confusion were targeted and shot down by machine guns and mortar fire.

"If we stay here, we'll die for sure."

"I know," Sergeant Aoki replied. "However . . ."

"What shall we do, Sergeant?"

The sergeant was silent. They were unable to escape. The shelling continued from morning to night without stopping. All around, the sound of exploding hand grenades marked the spot where another person had chosen an "honorable" death over capture of defeat by the enemy. Beneath the cliffs on the shore, the bodies of those who had thrown themselves to their death had begun to pile up.

Even after sundown, the American forces did not cut back on the shelling and bombardment. Their continuous flare bombs made night raids by their enemies impossible. Already the Japanese troops had no semblance of organized fighting power left. If they received an all-out attack from the U.S. forces, there was no way they could survive. Sergeant Aoki cast a somber glance at the mountaintop where the U.S. troops were and murmured, "Those guys will probably invade tomorrow."

"Aoki-san, if we stay here, we'll just be killed."

"This is the end."

"Let's get out of here."

"Get out? How?"

"We'll swim."

"Swim?"

"We'll swim around the rear of the enemy at Matansa."

The sergeant looked at Saburo with somber eyes and shook his head. "I can't swim for very long with this wound."

"If we stay here, we'll die for sure."

"You go on. I'll stay here. I'll take my life honorably here."

"Aoki-san! I'll help you swim. Let's go together!"

The sergeant said nothing.

"Haven't we managed to survive until now together, Aoki-san?"

"You go."

"I can't leave you here!"

"I'm finished."

"We live together or we die together. Come on, let's go together."

Sergeant Aoki didn't answer.

Saburo untied the gaiters from his legs.

"Give me yours, Aoki-san."

"What are you doing?"

"Tying the four of them together to make a rope. Here, tie one end to the belt around your waist. I'll pull you as I swim."

Sergeant Aoki stared at Saburo silently. Then his eyes filled with tears, and he gripped Saburo's hand. "Thank you!"

They stood on Marpi Point. Tracer rounds continued to crisscross the moonlit ocean. Among the waves, they could see the forms of countless people swimming. Saburo dove into the ocean. Sergeant Aoki followed. Saburo swam desperately, tightly gripping the makeshift rope and pulling the sergeant along.

As they swam, they realized that most of those they had thought to be swimmers among the waves were actually corpses adrift at sea. They swam westward, dodging bodies. Flare bombs illuminated the surface of the ocean. U.S. naval vessels offshore added their fire, and when flare bombs illuminated the surface of the ocean, Saburo dove into the masses of bodies. With only his face above water, he pretended to be a corpse until it was possible to swim on.

After some thirty minutes of being pounded by the waves, Sergeant Aoki looked like he was in agony.

"Come on, you can do it!" Saburo encouraged him.

Aoki gasped for air, engulfed by a wave. "I'm finished. Just let me go."

A little ways off shore, Saburo saw waves that were shattering in white foam against a reef. If they could make it to the rocks, they could catch their breath.

"Aoki-san, just to those rocks!"

Pulling Aoki with all his strength, Saburo swam toward the reef. Aoki could barely help now. Saburo's arms and legs were also beginning to feel heavy. If his strength gave out now, they would drown. Terror began to overpower him. But they were getting closer to the reef. "We're almost there!"

At that moment, a giant wave crashed over them. Saburo's body was sucked into the pitch-black of the ocean. Gasping for air, he took in water. Splitting pain washed over him. *I'm going to die!*

He struggled frantically, kicking his arms and legs desperately, and burst through the surface. With his head finally above water, he took in a deep breath. For a while he panted, adrift in the ocean. *Where's Aoki-san? No!*

The rope had slipped from his fingers.

"Aoki-san! Aoki-san!"

There was no sight of the sergeant. Saburo reached the reef and looked around, calling out for Aoki, but Aoki's voice did not answer. He had disappeared among the waves.

Saburo shivered. *Aoki-san is gone. He's dead.* Grief assailed him. He was lonely beyond words. *I'm all alone now. Am I going to die in this hellish ocean, too?*

As Saburo was tossed about by the waves, his thoughts turned dismal.

"Good luck, Saburo. Don't you die, now." Suddenly, the last words of his father, when they had parted at the dock at Tinian, rang in his ears. *That's right. Don't die now. Mustn't die.* Somehow, he found the strength to swim by himself. *I'll swim toward Matansa, as far as I can make it.*

After catching his breath and pulling himself together, Saburo swam out once again into the ocean among the dead bodies. From time to time, flare bombs exploded and heavy rifle shots fell on the ocean's surface. And each time, Saburo ducked under water and hid behind a corpse before continuing on.

Eventually, the eastern sky began to light up faintly. The black shape of Mount Marpi loomed to his left and behind him. *When morning comes, I'll be found. This is dangerous.* He knew he had to climb out onto the shore and plunge into the jungle while it was still dark.

Cautiously, he swam toward the sandy beaches that appeared to be Matansa. Countless bloated bodies that had begun to decompose floated in the water. Looking closer, he noticed several people swimming among them, with only their heads above water. They had probably leaped from Marpi Point and had swum all the way here. Saburo swam after them, as if he were in pursuit.

On the beach, he saw the forms of people milling about. *Enemy soldiers?* Suddenly tense, he kept an eye on them from his position among the waves. Then relief. . . . *They're allies!*

Discovering that the people on the beach were Japanese soldiers, Saburo climbed out of the ocean onto the land. Beneath some trees on the beach were about twenty young soldiers and civilians who had escaped from Marpi Point. They lay on their sides, dripping wet. Catching his breath, Saburo looked around for familiar faces, but found none. An elderly man spoke in a low voice, "It's dangerous to stay here. While it's still night, let's escape into the mountains."

Everyone complied silently and followed the elderly man's instructions. They began to walk toward the mountain, their forms stooped. Saburo followed at the tail end of the group. The area was pockmarked with holes from the bombing. Suddenly, nearly stepping on the form of a person lying on the ground, Saburo stopped dead in his tracks. The stench of the dead body pierced his nostrils. Straining his eyes, he looked about and saw countless bodies of soldiers lying scattered about, crumpled one over another—some glaring up at the heavens, eyes bulging with rage; some with limbs that had been torn off; others with horrible gaping wounds. This must be the scene of the Banzai charge. Saburo swallowed hard, and a chill crept up his spine.

"Hurry up!" a voice ordered. And at the same instant, machine gun fire broke loose. Bullets were flying everywhere, and Saburo watched people being bowled over backward, their bodies shattered. He leaped into a hole carved into the ground by an exploding shell. Bullets mowed down the grass and trees around him.

I can't stay here! Saburo jumped out of his hiding place and dashed for the jungle, running like a wild animal.

Chapter 8

Hiding in the Jungle

On the way back to the hotel in Garapan from the cliffs at Marpi, Pastor Arakaki stopped the car at Matansa and got out to walk toward the beach. Pushing past the brush at Adan, he stood on the white sand.

A sudden chill sea breeze carried the roar of the ocean washing up on the reef along the shore. The rusted, decayed remains of a boat lay half-buried in the sand. Otherwise, it was just a tranquil, beautiful beach. No one else was in sight. The sun sank into the west, where rain clouds billowed.

Silently and with a faraway look, Pastor Arakaki turned his eyes to the cliffs of Marpi about three miles (five kilometers) to the northeast.

"On that night, you swam in this very ocean, didn't you?" Miike asked.

Pastor Arakaki nodded without a word. The expression on his face was terse. He gazed into the sky. "This is a scary place," he said, deep in reverie.

In a U.S. military documentary photo, Miike had seen the bodies of Japanese soldiers after the banzai charge, lying strewn across Matansa's white sand, turning it black with decomposed corpses. Perplexed at how to dispose of them, the American troops had used a bulldozer to bury the bodies.

Pastor Arakaki pointed to the mountain in the east. "I escaped into the mountains somewhere around there."

The all-out attack, just before daybreak on July 7, brought organized battle by the Saipan garrison to an end. In the banzai charge, up to four thousand men died, including civilians. With the Marine Corps conquest of Marpi Point, the U.S. forces declared possession of Saipan.

"Japanese soldiers, Japanese soldiers, the war is already over. The U.S. forces have taken control of the island of Saipan. Japanese soldiers in the jungle and in the caves, surrender yourselves. Come out quickly, and raise your hands above your head." On July 7, using loudspeakers, the U.S. forces began to urge the Japanese to surrender.

"You will no longer face death. The American army will not kill you. Surrender yourselves. Come out, with your hands above your head. We will give you food. Hurry up and come out with your hands above your head."

Hiding in the brush of the mountainside jungle, Saburo kept an eye on the movements of the American forces. "As if I would give myself up," he spit out the words under his breath. Having narrowly escaped death when the Americans attacked Matansa, Saburo wandered about the jungle; after a while he ran into a small group of stragglers from the defeated Japanese troops. The group was headed for the summit of Tapotchau. The soldiers said they had met a surviving officer who had instructed them to join and fight with what was left of the army at Tapotchau. They all hung on to their last hope—that the combined fleet was on its way to save them.

"If you were a student at the Saipan Vocational School, you must know a lot about the geography, right?" They urged Saburo to lead the way. By day they hid in the brush and in caves and scouted out the movements of the U.S soldiers. After nightfall, they moved north toward Tapotchau.

From time to time, rifle shots reverberated all around. The U.S. forces had entered the jungle to annihilate the remaining Japanese troops. The hunted could not let down their guard for even a moment. Here and there lay the corpses of Japanese soldiers, giving off a terrible stench. Leaves had been blasted off the trees in the shelling, and the face of the mountain lay battered. It was as if the landscape itself had been altered.

Listening carefully, always on the watch, they walked by starlight through the dimly lit mountainside. Saburo's night vision was like that of a wild beast. "This is Telegraph Mountain," he announced.

"Oh, the area where there used to be a wireless telegraph office?"

"That's right. Down there to the west is Tanapag Harbor." The words were exchanged quietly.

"We're maybe halfway to Tapotchau."

"How far do you think we'll be able to go before daybreak?"

Mount Tapotchau was located slightly south of the island's center. His eyes shining brightly in the darkness, Saburo walked in the lead.

What's that? Saburo froze in his footsteps. A wire was strung between the trees. Before Saburo could warn him, one of the soldiers reached out to touch the wire. Somewhere, a metallic ringing sounded. Suddenly, thirty meters ahead, a machine gun burst into life and bullets came ripping through the darkness. Rifle shots rang out. Soldiers began falling to the ground with a thud. At the first ring of the trap, Saburo had instantly dropped to the ground; tracer after tracer skimmed past his head, and the ground around him spit dust as bullets struck. The U.S. troops had installed a trip-wire warning system and had been waiting for them. The storm of bullets raged all around for a long moment. A dying soldier called out for his mother. Saburo didn't move. Finally, the shooting died down, but Saburo still held his breath, playing dead. The U.S. forces were listening carefully for any movement in the area. But they didn't advance. Perhaps they were bracing for a counterattack; perhaps they were waiting for their next prey. Whatever the reason, the U.S. troops did not press the attack.

Still staying flat to the ground, Saburo inched his way backward and slipped into the brush to escape. All the Japanese soldiers in the group had been wiped out. Perhaps it was destiny, but time and again, Saburo faced imminent death—and barely escaped. But how long would he manage to survive? The future was even more perilous than the present. All alone once again, Saburo trudged through the darkness toward Tapotchau. What could he do but keep on walking?

He met from time to time with survivors—soldiers and civilians—wandering north and south on the mountainside. Most of the soldiers were headed for Tapotchau, and Saburo joined another group of a dozen or so. There seemed to be a vague notion of uniting at Tapotchau to prepare for a counterattack.

Meanwhile, there was imminent danger of being wiped out by the Americans positioned on the mountain ridges in view. The defeated soldiers avoided traveling in valleys and below cliffs because the U.S. forces could drop hand grenades on them. Tanks positioned on the roads on level ground tracked their movements.

Three or four days had passed since the banzai charge. A Japanese soldier relayed the news that several hundred civilians and soldiers had been taken prisoner at Banadero.

"Shame on them! What a disgrace!" Saburo muttered reflexively.

Once again, the ring of automatic rifles firing in rapid successions echoed across the mountainside. With each wave of bullets, more soldiers were shot to the ground. That day, Saburo and his comrades hid motionless in caves and in the thicket of the jungle. As the sun set, the gunfire seemed to cease. The American soldiers pulled back into their camps. After waiting for night to fall, Saburo and his comrades began to move. Searching for food along the way, they headed for Tapotchau, weaving their way between the hillside trees.

Suddenly the soldier in the lead threw himself flat on the ground. "The enemy!" he shouted.

Saburo and the other soldiers spread out among the trees and hid. But it was already too late. A platoon of American soldiers lined up along the road in the valley below, the muzzles of their guns pointing toward them. Saburo's group had surprised some U.S. soldiers heading back to their camp from the mop-up operation. One, who was apparently the leader, shouted an order in English, and a storm of bullets flew from their rifles in unison. More gunfire rained down from the ridge behind them. There was no path of retreat.

The Japanese soldiers who were armed returned fire. It was nothing compared to the overwhelming power of the U.S. forces, however. The Japanese threw their hand grenades, but they struck trees and exploded harmlessly without reaching the enemy.

Saburo was hiding in the shelter of a boulder, shaking. He had no weapon and could only lie there and watch, holding his head in his hands. Then in front of his eyes, a soldier who had been firing his rifle from behind a tree was shot. He bowled over backward and died instantly.

The Japanese rifles gradually fell silent as they ran out of ammunition.

Seeing that the Japanese resistance had weakened, the U.S. troops advanced toward them, firing at random. There was no way to escape.

Should I come out with my hands raised? Saburo asked himself. *Would I be shot? Taken prisoner? But I must never be taken prisoner!*

Saburo had no rifle. Not even a sword. Was he to expose himself to the enemy and choose honorable death?

In and out of sight among the trees, the U.S. troops approached until they stood only twenty or thirty meters away. Saburo's heart leaped wildly in his chest, and his entire body shook.

At that moment, a young Japanese soldier jumped to his feet. "Farewell, comrades!" he yelled at the top of his lungs and began running toward the surprised Americans. The gunfire zeroed in on him. As he collapsed in front of the U.S. soldiers, two hand grenades exploded.

Screams erupted from the U.S. troops. Yelling loudly, they retreated in confusion.

Saburo was dumbfounded. The Americans were gone, and the gunfire from behind had died away. Stillness returned to the area. Of the dozen or so of his buddies, more than half had died. But strangely enough, once again Saburo had survived. The death of the young soldier who had thrown himself forward as a sacrifice to the enemy had saved Saburo's life. His heart ached with gratitude.

Along with the four soldiers that remained, Saburo finally found his way to the western slopes of Tapotchau. Many remnant soldiers and civilians—easily more than a thousand—hid all over what was commonly called Coffee Mountain. After all he had been through, Saburo was stunned at the sheer number.

Here and there in the jungle, the men broke up into smaller groups. A few erected tents; some even dragged out galvanized sheets from the burnt debris of homes and constructed small shelters. For the most part, hand grenades were the only weapons they carried. The Japanese were essentially without fighting power. Several days passed. As Saburo was walking through the jungle during full daylight, a voice suddenly called out from the bushes.

"Hey, isn't that Arakaki? Saburo …?"

Saburo turned around, and a young man climbed out from the brush, his intense eyes shining. He was pale and emaciated and wrapped in tattering clothing. For a split second, Saburo wondered who it could possibly be. Then he rushed to the young man. "Hey! Toma!" Saburo thumped him on the back.

"You're alive, Saburo?"

It was Ryotoku Toma, a classmate from Saipan Vocational School. He, too, was originally from Okinawa.

"I thought it was you, Arakaki. But with that beard, I wasn't sure at first!" Toma's eyes shone, and Saburo grasped his hands, overjoyed at their reunion.

"So you came through alive, Toma!"

Toma had been unable to escape to Marpi Point and, dodging the U.S. troops, had hidden in Mount Tapotchau.

Soon after the two sat down in the brush and began talking, the sound of speakers reverberated from below in the jungle. "Japanese soldiers! Make yourselves known! All Japanese, come out, everyone! Don't be afraid! Come on out! Many, many of your friends have come to the camps. We have water and food. We have cigarettes. We have everything there." An American soldier shouted out over the loudspeakers in Japanese with a strange accent.

The two young men looked at each other. Fear flickered across Toma's face. Saburo muttered, "I won't be tricked. Not me!"

Toma's eyes clouded, and he said nothing.

"If you don't want to die, come out with your hands high over your head! Come to where the flag with the green cross flies! The Japanese Bushido didn't say for you to die like dogs. When you're dead, it's really over. Those who don't want to live, just stay there. The American army will attack. Those who don't want to die, come out with your hands over your heads. Hurry up and come out!"

Not a single person attempted to surrender.

"We're Japanese! We won't suffer the shame of being taken alive as prisoners. Right, Toma?" Saburo looked at Toma with a fierce look in his eyes.

Toma nodded weakly without meeting Saburo's gaze. "But, you know, Saburo, I . . . I don't want to die."

Morning dawned, and by the following morning, most of the refugees who had been all over Coffee Mountain had disappeared. They had apparently descended the mountain under the cover of night and surrendered to the U.S. troops.

Three days later, the U.S. forces came with a violent mop-up operation. Saburo managed to survive, but Ryotoku Toma was shot down in a shower of bullets.

Looking into the lifeless face of his school buddy, Saburo couldn't let himself cry. *Sooner or later, it will be me,* he thought. *Sleep on, Toma. Rest in peace.*

He was alone again. Rather than feeling despair, however, Saburo now felt an intense fury in his heart.

The U.S. mop-up operation intensified as the day progressed. In the jungle, the bodies of the newly dead accumulated. On Mount Tapotchau, a number of small groups of armed soldiers continued to fearlessly return fire against the U.S. forces. But the Americans always retaliated in force. Most of the civilians who remained in the mountainside to avoid the enemy eventually descended from the mountain, surrendered, and were taken into custody by the U.S. Army. A civilian detention camp was set up at Susupe.

While wandering about the mountainside, Saburo encountered a group of about fifty armed men under the leadership of Army Captain Sakae Oba. They were surviving commissioned and noncommissioned officers as well as enlisted men from both the army and the navy. These men were too proud to be taken as prisoners and planned to cooperate with the Japanese combined fleet when it counterattacked and recaptured Saipan. Saburo decided to throw in his lot with them.

In the group was MP Corporal Takeo Jojima, who demonstrated an undefeated attitude. At twenty-one, he was a young, spirited noncommissioned officer only three years older than Saburo. Now he was Saipan's one and only remaining MP. He was single-handedly spying on the movements of the American forces and researching their psychological state by infiltrating the civilian detention camp at Susupe and making contact with volunteers there. He was always racking his brains trying to figure out the movements of the Americans and how to conduct guerrilla warfare against them.

"What are they like, those Yankees?" Saburo asked him.

"They don't even have the courage to sacrifice themselves for their country," Jojima replied. "We, on the other hand, are ready to lay ourselves aside for the Divine Emperor and our nation. In the end, we will triumph—without doubt."

Jojima spoke earnestly of the strength and dignity of the Japanese spirit. His intrepid vision and self-confidence captured Saburo.

"A time for revenge will come," he continued. "We must prepare for that day." Saburo worshiped the young MP's fierce fighting spirit and his unrelenting loyalty to the emperor.

I wouldn't mind dying, if it was with this person, Saburo thought. He trusted Jojima to that extent. From then on, Saburo acted on the orders of MP Corporal Takeo Jojima. He was soon handed a rifle that had been abandoned by the U.S. troops. With high spirits and with rifle in hand, Saburo began to enthusiastically take part in armed skirmishes. Along with the soldiers, he raided American food dumps that were short on guards and robbed them clean of food such as cans of corned beef.

It was also Saburo who, under the cover of night, dragged back a cow that had escaped from its pasture. When it came time to kill it for food, none of the soldiers wanted to lay a hand on it, perhaps fearing a curse. Saburo laughed. "I can do it," he said. He picked up his rifle, pointed it between the cow's eyebrows, and casually killed it. Nothing bothered his conscience. He had no respect for anything.

One night, as the men were roasting African snails in a cave in the valley, they found themselves surrounded by U.S. troops. When they realized it, it was already too late to escape. The Americans opened fire, and all the soldiers around Saburo were shot to death. Saburo was hit in the lower right jaw, but undaunted, he managed to escape, leaping from boulder to boulder.

He faced death constantly, but by some good fortune, he always escaped by the skin of his teeth. Saburo tenaciously survived on Mount Tapotchau for more than a year until the end of the war. The wound in his jaw had healed by then.

Chapter 9

Assassination Order

On the morning of the second day of the journey the car carrying the entire troupe exited the hotel at Garapan and headed south along the mountainside Middle Road.

The group was searching for the remains of the civilian detention camp at Susupe where Pastor Arakaki had committed his first murder. Today, forty-two years later, he was to visit that very spot again.

Words between Pastor Arakaki and Miike dwindled. Cameraman Mitsuoka intently filmed the expression on Pastor Arakaki's face. Sound technician Amata was not his usual witty self. Aware of the heavy atmosphere in the car, Director Imura at the wheel attempted to break the tension by commenting on the weather.

Only four days and three nights had been scheduled for filming and data collection in Saipan. With a total of ten short days for the entire trip, including filming in Guam and Hawaii, the schedule was inflexible. There was no room to make up even a single day's work.

The car followed a winding road past a memorial honoring Saipan's residents on the left. Soon, a building appeared on the right side.

"That must be the North Mariana Union Headquarters," Miike said, looking at his map.

Pastor Arakaki pointed to the grove of palm trees and South Sea pines to the left. "Lake Susupe should be beyond there."

To the right of the road was the back of a bustling row of buildings along the shorefront beach road. Single-story homes stood among the fields. Pastor Saburo tilted his head slightly. "I remember that the Japanese civilian detention camp was somewhere around here in Susupe. . . . Things have really changed."

Miike glanced at Pastor Arakaki with a flicker of apprehension. Pastor Arakaki gazed intently ahead. The car continued toward the south for a while.

"Stop the car," Pastor Arakaki said. He scratched his head. He looked intently to his left and right and murmured, "This is Chalan Kanoa. This is where the islander's camp was. Turn around."

Imura made a U-turn.

After they had retraced their route a short while, Pastor Arakaki stopped the car once again, stepped out, and took off at a quick pace. Cameraman Mitsuoka frantically trailed after him. Miike followed. Pastor Arakaki grabbed a passerby and asked, "Do you know where the Japanese camp was . . . forty-two years ago?"

"Sorry." The passerby looked puzzled. Pastor Arakaki asked person after person, but no one seemed to know.

"But there must be at least one or two people who know about that time," Pastor Arakaki walked restlessly about. Dogs in the neighborhood began to bark incessantly, throwing everything into a commotion.

In an attempt to completely take out the Japanese waterfront position, the U.S. forces had shelled the area from their warships. Even today, some houses have gate posts made of huge unexploded shells!

By the end of the war, fifteen thousand Japanese civilians from the surrounding area were interned by the Americans. A barbed wire fence had encircled the camp. He could find the site of the first murder, Pastor Arakaki said, only by finding the south end of that fence and using that as a starting point. Had that plan failed? By now there were no remains of the fence to be found anywhere.

Pastor Arakaki stopped in his tracks. He paused in the middle of the road under the sweltering sun and stared at his surroundings.

* * * * *

Saburo stood alone on the tableland at the southwest foot of Tapotchau. The soldiers called this plateau No. 2 Rail, because from there, at some three hundred feet above sea level, they could see the No. 2 Light Rail of the sugar mill leading to the sea. Standing there on this day in the middle of August 1945, Saburo could see—beyond Cape Agingan on the island's southern tip—the outline of Tinian Island.

After the suicidal charge by Saipan's garrison, the U.S. forces invaded Tinian Island. The veil of gunpowder smoke that lay over the island and the thundering echo of bombing testified to the severity of the battle there. The battle was over in only a week or so. Tinian's garrison had probably mounted a banzai charge as well, Saburo decided. He thought of his father in Tinian.

I wonder if he's alive. Dad, I hope you're still alive. I'm still alive, Saburo called out toward Tinian in his heart.

After the U.S. occupation, silver B-29 Super Fortress bombers, larger than any Saburo had ever seen, flew by the hundreds from Aslito Airbase and Tinian Island's airfield toward the north. "They're probably on their way to carry out air raids on the Japanese mainland," someone suggested. Now, however, even that seemed to have stopped. The island was quiet.

The Americans continued to urge the Japanese to surrender. The loudspeaker messages claimed that Japan had surrendered, but few were lured out. From No. 2 Rail, they could see American jeeps and trucks running incessantly along Garapan's seaside road. Warships lay anchored at open sea, but the signs of severe, violent battle had vanished.

Farther south on the slope where Saburo stood was farmland where the prisoners in the civilian detention camp grew vegetables. The straggler soldiers on the mountain, who continued their guerilla combat, raided the farm grounds by night and stole potatoes, tomatoes, and cucumbers. The farm grounds were also where the soldiers met secretly with prisoners who supported their guerrilla warfare. Food, medicine, and information regarding the U.S. military were thus conveyed to the mountain, and weapons were smuggled into the detention camp. The man who established this underground route was MP Corporal Takeo Jojima.

Beyond the farmland, in the shade of groves of South Sea Pines, Saburo could see the tents and barracks of the detention camp.

Why did I raise my hand just like that and volunteer to infiltrate the camp? The thought still bothered Saburo.

On Mount Tapotchau, in the area that was commonly called Mount Tako, Jojima had called Saburo aside. "Arakaki, listen up. I want you to infiltrate the camp."

"What? Did you say, infiltrate? No way! Not in my lifetime! I could never do that!" Saburo refused.

"Listen, Arakaki. The U.S. forces have started a false rumor in the camp that Japan has surrendered. Some Japanese have started wavering and are ready to side with the Americans."

"What? What kind of Japanese would do that?"

"There's also a rumor that the emperor has gone to battle."

"It's almost time for the counterattack, isn't it?"

"There's no proof. The refugees are confused. At this rate, the number of those who side with the U.S. will only increase. If that happens, our counterattack plan will fail—even with help from within the camps. Relief for those of us still in the mountains will stop. You understand what that means, don't you, Arakaki?"

"Yes, sir."

"So, you *will* infiltrate the camp."

"What do you mean?"

"Afterwards, I'll infiltrate, too. I'll say I'm a student of the Saipan Vocational School."

"What?"

"Then, you will testify that I am a classmate of yours from school."

Saburo nodded.

"Now, listen, Arakaki. There's something we have to do while we are inside the camp. It's for the emperor, for the Divine Nation."

"I'm infiltrating for the emperor, for the Divine Nation?"

"That's right. You'll do it?"

"Yes . . . I'll do it."

Saburo had vowed in his heart to live or die with MP Corporal Jojima. Partly because of that vow, Saburo felt obligated to do as he was asked—even to the point of allowing himself to become a prisoner in order to infiltrate the camp. It was all a part of their scheme.

And so Saburo had emerged from the brush of No. 2 Rail and

descended the slope to the farming grounds with both hands raised above his head.

Two American soldiers quickly spotted him and drove up in a jeep. At Saburo's first close-up look at the reddish faces of the American soldiers, tension and hatred rose in his heart. One of them leveled a rifle at him. They searched him for weapons.

"Are you a soldier?"

"No. Saipan schoolboy."

"OK."

The search ended rather quickly.

Saburo was taken to a Quonset building that seemed to be the mop-up operation headquarters.

What's going to happen to me? Suppressing his anxiety, Saburo scrutinized his surroundings. A group of African-American soldiers was eating. One of them smiled, showing a row of white teeth. He walked over to Saburo with a sandwich and a mug of coffee in his hands.

For me?

The act of kindness was unexpected, but Saburo was suspicious. *You think you'll win me over?* The soldier laughed and motioned for Saburo to eat.

Saburo's stomach couldn't resist for long. Much to his chagrin, Saburo gave in and devoured the sandwich.

In a separate room, a second-generation Japanese-American questioned Saburo—full name, age, occupation.

"I'm a third-year student at Saipan Vocational School," Saburo answered.

"Hang on a minute," the Japanese-American said. A Japanese man was called in from outside.

"Hey!" Saburo called out without thinking when he saw the man. It was Isamu Sakiyama, his classmate from the vocational school. He and Saburo had been separated on the day the U.S. forces had invaded the island.

Sakiyama was equally surprised to see Saburo.

"Sakiyama, do you know this man?" the Japanese-American asked.

"Yes. It's Saburo Arakaki. He's a classmate of mine from Saipan Vocational School."

"Do you so testify?"

"Yes. Without a doubt."

"OK."

The questioning was over, and Saburo had his picture taken for an ID card. He was placed in bachelor housing.

Fifteen thousand Japanese were in the camp. Amazingly enough, a school for the children and even a Japanese police organization had already been set up. A barbed wire fence surrounded the camp. Saipanese guards policed the area beyond the gates and fence.

The prisoners were divided into ten groups. Each group shared tents and barracks. The adults were sent out to work on tasks assigned by the labor section. Sakiyama, who had quickly surrendered to the U.S. forces on Tapotchau, did miscellaneous chores in the office area.

"Arakaki, you've done well to stay alive," Sakiyama spoke with nostalgia. Three other classmates from Saipan Vocational School were in the camp, he said.

"Sakiyama, I have a favor to ask of you," Saburo whispered. Seeing the serious look on Saburo's face, Sakiyama looked at him questioningly.

"There's another person coming into the camp—one of us from the school. His name's Ryotoku Toma."

"Toma! So he's alive, too?"

"Toma was shot to death."

"What? So . . ."

"It's someone else. From the military."

Sakiyama was silent.

"If you're asked, our stories should match. And tell them to call me. I'll testify to his identity."

"All right," Sakiyama nodded, and Saburo pressed his case.

"Don't let me down. It's someone important."

Three days later, MP Corporal Takeo Jojima, disguised as a civilian, infiltrated the camp. Perhaps Sakiyama wasn't around at the time, but Saburo was called into the cross-examination room.

"Hey, Toma!" Saburo called out when he saw Jojima. The Japanese-American looked closely at Saburo and questioned him. "Do you know this man?"

"Yes. He's Ryotoku Toma. He's a classmate."

Jojima passed the investigation without any difficulty and was placed in the same bachelor quarters as Saburo. That night, Saburo had Sakiyama round up their classmates. They were Choyu Shimabukuro, Shohei Ota, and Katsuo Yamashiro. They were old buddies and were thrilled to see one another again.

Yamashiro spoke. "Saburo, Churyo said you saved him."

"Oh, how is he doing?"

In the mop-up operations by U.S. forces, an underclassman from his hometown, Churyo Tamanaha, had been badly wounded in both legs by a fragment of trench mortar. With their movement hindered in the jungle, the soldiers couldn't manage to carry the boy who was pale from loss of blood; neither could they just leave him there. They had ordered Saburo to kill him.

"No way! I can't!"

"It's better to kill him. It's called compassion."

"Let me decide what to do with him."

"What are you going to do?"

"I'll have him taken as a prisoner."

As the soldiers watched in surprise, Saburo hoisted Churyo on his back and slowly descended thirty meters down a steep cliff. He then crossed through the jungle and set Churyo down a mere hundred meters from the American troops.

"Churyo, listen to me. I'm going back. Wait half an hour until I've climbed back up the cliff. Then call loudly for help. The U.S. troops will hear you and come looking for you. You're just a kid. They won't kill you. They'll nurse your wounds. You'll be saved."

"Saburo-san!" Churyo's eyes filled with tears.

"Don't cry. See you!"

Now, Saburo learned that Churyo, whom he had left there like that, was alive.

"Man, you're amazing, Saburo."

Saburo's buddies showered him with praise. He laughed lightheartedly. "Anyway, I really need to ask a favor of you guys."

Saburo brought Jojima forward. "This man is Ryotoku Toma."

"Ryotoku Toma? Give me a break!" Shimabukuro burst into laughter. Saburo spoke in a restrained voice.

"Listen carefully. This man's real name is . . ."

"Jojima," Jojima spoke up.

"He's an MP," Saburo said.

"What!"

Shimabukuro fell silent, and his nervous glance fell on Jojima.

"In order to carry out an important assignment, he lied about his identity to infiltrate this camp. From now on, call him Toma."

"Comrades, please cooperate with me," Jojima looked at the circle of faces around him.

"We are fighting for the day of total uprising on the island when our allies will counterattack. We have already stocked up arms in this camp for that day. I want all of you to support us."

Ota and Yamashiro glanced at each other.

"Japan will never lose. In the end she will surely triumph. If ever, now is the time when our love for our nation will pull us through to victory," Jojima said. He looked around with a stern expression, then continued, "Right now, in this very camp, some people are spreading false rumors that Japan has lost the war. This is an unforgivable act for a Japanese to commit."

"Unforgivable!" Saburo spat out in hatred.

Ota nodded. "That's right."

"We can't let them get away with this," Jojima insisted.

"What are we going to do?" asked Sakiyama.

"We'll silence them. If they don't respond to threats, we'll punish them." Jojima's piercing eyes captured the hearts of the young men. Their eyes shone, and they nodded enthusiastically.

Other soldiers had also infiltrated the camp pretending to be civilians. The American forces and civilian police were searching for these counterfeit civilians. Several had already been caught; it was said that they had been marched on foot to the prisoner's camp at Matansa.

Because most of the infiltrators were in the bachelor quarters, Saburo looked for a way to be housed elsewhere and avoid discovery. He learned that a couple who had helped him out in Garapan—Mr. and Mrs. Miyagi—were being held in Group #5 housing. He asked the Miyagis to allow him and Jojima to stay with them for a while. They were overjoyed to learn that Saburo was alive, and they welcomed him and Jojima to stay with them.

Saburo and Jojima worked on the farming grounds during the day. By night, they secretly gathered together with the other confederates to talk things over. Night after night, Jojima preached his conviction that Japan would be victorious in the end. He had quite a following among the young men. The camp was divided between "the loser's party," who acknowledged Japan's defeat, and "the winner's party," who denied that Japan could ever be conquered.

At night, the U.S. forces showed news films in the camp commons—scenes of Americans celebrating victory, Tokyo as a burnt field after the air raids, and American troops advancing across the screen. Most of the prisoners crowded together and watched the films, clearly agitated. The "loser's party" began to grow in strength. The leader of that group declared, "Japan has lost. Tojo has deceived us. Our emperor who declared war on America made a grave mistake. Now more than ever, it is the time for us to crush the old feudalism and create a new Japan."

"Traitor!"

"Traitor to Japan!"

"Disloyal Japanese!"

Protests rose in the air, but they were drowned in the angry roar of other voices, "Give it up!"

"You don't understand a thing!"

Meanwhile, at night Jojima continued to arouse the patriotism of the young men—either former soldiers or those who had been students of the Saipan Vocational School. At the same time, he fanned their hatred of the "loser's party." They sent an anonymous threatening note to the four leaders of the "loser's party": "Refrain from the disgraceful speech and conduct of traitors. Otherwise, consider yourselves dead."

However, nothing really happened. Day by day, the view that Japan had indeed been defeated gained momentum. A former civilian employee for the army, a Mr. Asai (not his real name), was even receiving preferential treatment after becoming a group leader in the U.S. forces work operation. This enraged Jojima and the young men in his group.

Standing in front of the young men, maddened with enthusiasm, Jojima declared quietly, "We'll teach them a lesson. First of all, we'll assassinate that American stooge, Mr. Asai."

The young men swallowed hard and exchanged looks.

"It's for the Divine Emperor, for the Divine Nation."

Jojima scanned the circle of young faces. His glance fell on Saburo. "You have courage, Arakaki. You do it."

Chapter 10

Murder!

Pastor Arakaki shut his eyes against the blazing sunlight. It looked as if he might be praying. Miike obligingly stood at a distance. They could hear the voices of children playing not too far away. Pastor Arakaki began to walk in that direction, as if drawn by their voices. As they followed the alley, they came upon a small open lot. The children were playing with water. An elderly woman sat in a chair beneath the eaves of a nearby house, watching the children, a smile on her face. The pastor approached her.

"Hello. Are you from Chamorro?"

"Yes. Are you Japanese?" the woman answered, smiling.

"Yes. I was a student at Saipan Vocational School." The pastor spoke cheerfully and with candor.

The woman began to speak in Japanese. "Is that so? I was taught by a Japanese teacher."

Oh? Before the war. I see."

"Are you from Tokyo?"

"Okinawa."

"Oh. There used to be plenty of people from Okinawa here."

"There used to be a Japanese camp here, right?"

"Yes, yes. I was in the Saipanese camp at Chalan Kanoa."

"You know, I'm looking for the ruins of the Japanese camp." Pastor Arakaki stooped down beside the elderly woman. "Where is the southern tip of the camp?" he asked.

"The southern tip? Agingan?"

"No, not the cape at Agingan. I mean, the southern tip of the camp. There used to be a barbed wire fence, right?"

"Yes, there was a fence."

"Do you know where it is?"

"Yes. Take the road that way," she pointed. "There are the remains of the gravesites there. Graves for Japanese who died in the camp. They moved the bones."

"I remember. The southern fence was by those graves. Outside of that, there was a road."

"Yes, that's right." The elderly woman nodded.

Pastor Arakaki extended his hand.

"Thank you. I appreciate it."

The elderly woman smiled back. Pastor Arakaki stood up, and as if suddenly remembering, he added, "By the way, do you know Jesus Guerrero? He was the police chief of the island before the war."

"He's my husband's cousin. I'm a Guerrero, too."

"Really?" Pastor Arakaki looked shocked.

"Jesus Guerrero died already. Almost ten years ago."

With this information as a guide, Pastor Arakaki walked briskly toward the east. On the left side of the road stood a single magnificent tree.

"That's an ironwood tree. I've seen it before. About a hundred meters to the east there should be a road that runs north and south."

"There is. Listen, you can hear cars," Miike said.

"The eastern fence ran along that road." Pastor Arakaki stopped in his tracks and pointed at the tree.

"I'm sure of it. Just north of that tree. Beyond the bushes. That's where the Miyagis' place was, where the MP and I stayed. We young men gathered together there at night. That's where I was given the assassination order."

"The MP ordered you to kill the leader of the 'loser's party'?"

"That's right. Not only me, but two others as well."

"All students of the Saipan Vocational School?"

"Yes. One was a former civilian employee in the army. He acted as the scout."

"The three of you . . . how did you go about it?"

The pastor's fierce gaze lay far beyond the tree.

"Following the MP's order, we secretly checked out Mr. Asai's barracks—Group #10—and hammered out an elaborate strategy. The assassination was to be carried out at midnight. At dusk on that day, the MP handed me a bayonet. The other two were handed rifles. If I failed, they would finish it up with the rifles."

"What were your feelings at that time?"

"I had mixed feelings. I was wavering. If it had come to this, that I had to kill somebody. . . . I'm sure anybody would be filled with anxiety and dread, with a tormented conscience. It was agony. But I shook off my conscience and insisted to myself, 'He's a traitor. You have to kill him. Just kill him. You're killing him for the Divine Emperor, for the Divine Nation.' That's how I hardened my determination."

The pastor's eyes grew dark. He was silent for a moment.

"One hour before executing our plan, the three of us sneaked out here and headed toward the house where Mr. Asai was."

Miike listened silently.

Pastor Arakaki began walking eastward. Miike followed. They emerged at the north-south road and turned left, then northward from where the eastern fence had stood. For ten minutes or so, they walked in silence in the scorching sun. Miike kept wiping at the sweat on his brow.

"Along a dark path on a starless night," Pastor Arakaki said suddenly as he walked. "The rest of the camp was fast asleep. . . ."

Miike was silent.

"We walked along, keeping watch on all sides. And I had such a heavy, gloomy feeling."

A grove of ironwood trees stood beside the road. "There it is, the grove of trees. . . . Yes, it's to the west of that," Pastor Arakaki murmured.

A narrow path cut through the grove, and Pastor Arakaki followed it. Miike checked to make sure the cameras were close behind and then proceeded in the pastor's footsteps.

They emerged from the grove onto an empty lot.

"It's the remains of the camp commons. Where they showed the films," Pastor Arakaki said. There was not a soul to be seen. To the west of the lot stood a small, uninhabited, single-story structure. To the northeast, they could see Mount Tapotchau. Less than a thousand feet farther to the west, Pastor Arakaki stopped in his tracks. "The barracks stood somewhere around here," he told Miike.

* * * * *

The three young men hid in the public bathrooms near the commons. They were very close to Mr. Asai's house. Saburo looked about with a watchful eye and waited for the moment of assassination. He couldn't restrain the pounding of his heart.

It was five minutes before the fateful hour of midnight. Saburo gripped the bayonet in his right hand. The two others released the safety locks on their rifles. Saburo's earlier wavering had vanished, and he was not afraid. A fiery impatience boiled within.

When the illuminated dial on the watch that they had borrowed from the MP read midnight, the three moved stealthily toward the designated house. One, carrying a rifle, approached the window; another stood near the doorway. Saburo moved toward the entrance and scouted out the inside of the building.

"All right!"

Firmly gripping the bayonet, Saburo motioned to the other two and opened the door. At that instant, one of his buddies flooded the room with his flashlight. They saw a man stand up. Saburo rushed at him at full speed and stabbed him with the bayonet. A moan rose in the air. In his boiling hatred, Saburo stabbed the man a second time. A warm substance coated Saburo's hand. The man fell to the floor.

"We did it." Saburo motioned to his buddies. As planned, the three split in different directions. At that moment, a powerful rain storm broke loose, erasing the sounds and the footsteps of the three fleeing men. Saburo stopped at the Group #7 public restroom and dropped the bloodstained weapon into the latrine.

MP Corporal Jojima was waiting at the #5 barracks. "Did you do it?"

"I did," Saburo answered.

The MP thumped Saburo on the shoulders. "Good job! You did great!"

The blood that dried on Saburo's hands didn't come off even when he washed.

* * * * *

Pastor Arakaki made a fist, as if he were holding a bayonet, and gazed at his hand. "With this hand . . . with this very hand, I killed him." His voice was heavy. No doubt, the memory was painful, for his face sank just slightly.

Miike didn't know what to say. Sadness welled up within.

"The final cry of that man who died . . . I can't forget it, even now." A shadow fell over the pastor's eyes as he blinked. From the side, the cameras heartlessly filmed the expression on his face. Miike's heart ached.

The pastor lowered his head. His eyes were closed. "I was totally in the wrong. Mr. Asai was, in fact, right. He recognized the reality of the situation. He didn't bow to pressure and persevered in believing what was right. I, on the other hand, didn't know left from right and was convinced that blindly following the MP's orders was for the sake of the Divine Emperor and the Divine Nation. And that's what led me to commit this offense. There is no sin more horrible than this."

His hands, held tightly together at his chest, trembled faintly. "All I can do now is seek forgiveness and pray that Mr. Asai's soul rests in peace. Please . . . please let me offer a prayer of repentance to God." Closing his eyes, he bowed his head and stood motionless, baring his soul before the camera. Tears fell from his closed eyes.

Miike was suddenly overcome by indescribably powerful emotions. Why had he made this man come here? He couldn't stop the tears that flowed from his own eyes.

Chapter 11

The Second Murder

The search for the second murder site was not going smoothly.

They were to enter the jungle, using as a guiding point the No. 2 Light Rail tableland at the southwest foot of Mount Tapotchau where Saburo had stood overlooking the civilian detention camp at Susupe that day he had surrendered to the Americans forty-two years earlier.

"First, I want to climb up there," Pastor Arakaki pointed. Gazing out from Susupe, the plateau appeared to be a gently sloping hill covered with brush, some three hundred feet high. It looked as though one could easily climb to the summit. The tableland at its base that had once been the farming grounds for the detention camp had since been turned into golf courses and housing. "There must be a road going up there."

Director Imura drove the car around, but there was no road to be found. The group wasted precious time driving back and forth. They asked passersby, but received only vague answers. The sun had already begun to dip westward, and Miike glanced at his wristwatch. "Isn't there a road that goes up there?"

"I think so, but . . ." Pastor Arakaki was at a loss. "Why don't we go to the summit of Tapotchau?" he said. "We can look for a road from the top."

Imura unfolded a map. "The road to the summit of Mount Tapotchau is on the map. Let's see how far we can get."

From Susupe toward the east of Mount Tapotchau, they began to glimpse Laulau Bay (also called Magicienne Bay) on the east side of the island. They continued north on the cross-island road. Miike was pondering how the trip would come across in a documentary. What would happen if they couldn't get to the second site? If they had to extend their stay in Saipan, their subsequent schedule in Guam and Hawaii would collapse. The schedule left no room for changes.

Ahead, on the left side of the road, a cross on a steeple appeared. Just then, the sound of bells floated out from the Catholic church. Its clear ringing instantly captured Miike's heart.

"I want that sound!" he said.

Imura slammed on the brakes. Mitsuoka rolled down the window and thrust the camera microphone out the window. The bells stopped ringing. At the same moment, a car honked behind them. Imura stuck his hand out the window and motioned for the car to go around them, but it didn't move. Instead, a man in uniform got out.

"Oh, no, it's a police officer!" Imura grimaced. Were they in trouble for coming to a sudden stop?

"Your identification papers, please," the officer said. Imura showed him his I-visa and press passport and managed to explain in English that they were a Japanese TV crew on location.

"Where are you headed?"

"The summit of Tapotchau."

"The mountain roads are very slick from the rains we've had recently."

"We can't go?"

The officer pointed to the car's tires.

"Not in this car."

Imura glanced back at the others in the back seat. Pastor Arakaki rolled down his window and stuck out his head.

"Hello. We want to go to the valley north of the Susupe golf course. The flatland. We don't know how to get to the road that takes us there."

"Oh," the officer laughed. "In that case, turn around. Just beyond the golf course, there's a road that goes off to the right. That's the road that goes up there."

"I see, I see. Thank you!" An elated Pastor Arakaki extended his hand to the police officer.

The police officer shook his hand, a smile on his face. "You're welcome."

Miike was relieved. What might have happened, he wondered, if they hadn't stopped and had kept on driving? In the settling twilight, they would have, no doubt, run into trouble and perhaps been stranded.

Imura turned the car around. They soon came to the golf course on the right-hand side of the road next to a grove of trees. As they took the curve that circled to the right, they saw a narrow road that ran between the trees. "That must be it," Imura murmured and steered the car to the right. The road quickly came to a dead end. There was a house and, straight ahead, the golf course fairway.

The staff reluctantly got out of the car. It was sundown, and not a single golfer was in sight. "Shall we cut across the green?"

"Yeah, if we go that far, maybe we'll see where to go on." They began to walk across the lawn. However, before they had gone a hundred feet, they were stopped by a shout.

"Hey! Where do you think you're going?" A man burst out of the house shouting angrily in Japanese.

For a split second, they all stood there frozen in their tracks. Pastor Arakaki promptly hurried toward the small-framed man in his sixties who looked somewhat like a Kanaka, or local native.

"Hello, friend!" Pastor Arakaki extended his hand. The man stopped in his tracks. "I'm a pastor. Pastor Arakaki. I was a student at Saipan Vocational School during the war."

"Is that so? I was a student at the boy's school." The silvery-haired man's expression softened, and he shook the pastor's hand.

"I fought against the American army," the pastor said.

The man responded, "I learned from Yamashiro-sensei, a military officer, how to fire a 38-caliber rifle. When the American forces were advancing, I said, 'Let me haul ammunition or whatever.' Yamashiro-sensei said, 'No way, you kids, go home to your parents.' "

"I see."

"He said a good thing. Otherwise, I'd be dead." The suntanned face opened up.

"Yes. That's good." Pastor Arakaki grasped the man's hand again.

"I'm Francisco. And you?" He looked at the staff. Imura greeted him and explained that they were a TV crew from Japan.

"Mr. Francisco, I was in the mountains with the Japanese army." Pastor Arakaki briefly explained the circumstances. "We want to go up to that plain, but we haven't been able to find the road."

"Oh, you can't get there from here. There's a road way over there that goes up. I'll take you tomorrow."

"Mr. Francisco, thank you."

Miike was relieved, but a puzzling emotion filled his heart. They had initially gotten lost—and even further lost. Then, somehow Francisco had appeared to guide the way.

The following morning, a man who appeared to be in his forties sat waiting for them in a jeep, along with Francisco. Large and muscular, he was bare to the waist. Francisco explained that the man was his cousin, Benancio, who was going to help them.

"I'm glad to have your help." Pastor Arakaki extended his hand. Benancio smiled, revealing a row of white teeth, and simply nodded.

The road to the plain north of Susupe was closer to Garapan than anyone had thought. It did run to the right, as the police officer had said, and it was very steep. After a while, the crew's station wagon slipped on the incline, unable to make it up the mountain. Transferring the cameras and equipment to Francisco's jeep, the group began to walk. The sun beat down on them.

The road ended at the tableland. There had been an attempt to construct a vista point for tourists, but Francisco said that it had been destroyed by a typhoon midconstruction, and those plans had been abandoned. Only the ruins remained.

Grass as tall as a man covered the gently sloping tableland. North and east lay a valley of jungle, and beyond that, Tapotchau's mountainside sloped up to the summit.

Pastor Arakaki looked around with a piercing glance, not saying a word. He nodded to himself now and then.

Francisco pointed to the valley in the east and said, "I came out from the valley over there to pick sugarcane, and that's when I was captured here by the Americans."

"So you know the geography of this area well."

"But it's changed. It used to be a bald mountain, laid bare by the war."

"Yes. Yes, but somewhere there must be remains of the old mountain road. Let's go northeast."

"OK." Francisco pointed the way to Benancio.

"Cameras ready?" Miike wanted to know. "OK, let's go."

Imura was the first to follow Benancio, who hacked a pathway through the grass. The choking smell of newly cut grass filled the air. Francisco, Pastor Arakaki, and Miike plowed through the grass. Mitsuoka and Amada followed, drenched in heavy sweat, trying to capture the expressions on Pastor Arakaki's face. A short distance in, the tall grass ended, and the jungle began.

"Let's go on," Pastor Arakaki said.

"There should be traces of the old road around here," Benancio said.

He was at the head of the group, cutting back the vines with a machete. With unbelievable agility for a man sixty years old, Pastor Arakaki ducked beneath the branches of large trees and stepped across fallen logs.

A large coconut crab was climbing a tree. "Luckily, Saipan doesn't have any poisonous snakes—unlike Okinawa." Miike dripped with perspiration, and he was beginning to feel out of breath.

"Look, pineapples!" Pastor Arakaki stopped in his tracks and pointed. Wild pineapple trees, covered with small fruit, were growing out of the ground.

"Here?" Miike was surprised.

The pastor took a pineapple in his hand. "During the war, the land was cultivated, and pineapples were planted all over. Those pineapples must have become wild."

Benancio split open the pineapple with his machete. The pastor slipped the small fruit into his mouth.

"Ahh. The taste of Saipan of forty-one years ago!" The pastor closed his eyes. "Let's stop and rest here a while."

Imura agreed and set down the heavy equipment that rested on his shoulder. Everyone was short of breath. Benancio passed out pieces of pineapple. The tangy-sweet natural fruit juice moistened their throats. Hearing an unusual birdcall, Miike looked up into the treetops and discovered a pure white tropical bird with long tail feathers circling in the sky above. After a short rest, the troupe resumed the trek through the jungle.

"Mr. Francisco, let's go a little farther. I'm looking for a cave in the valley that we used to cook in. If we can find that, we're OK."

Francisco nodded to Pastor Arakaki and called out to Benancio.

Benancio silently slashed away with his machete, clearing a path.

The jungle brush thickened, and it became difficult to move forward. The cameras were falling behind. But they pressed on.

Pastor Arakaki stopped from time to time to look in all four directions. They were approaching the summit of Tapotchau. To the left, they could see the valley.

"No. Let's go farther to the right," Pastor Arakaki said, and Francisco passed the word along to Benancio. They had been walking in the jungle for almost an hour.

"Mr. Miike!" Pastor Arakaki suddenly called out. "Doesn't this look like the remains of an old road?" The spot he pointed to certainly looked like it had once been a small path. However, it was narrow and became swallowed up in the jungle after a few meters. But it definitely wasn't a path used by animals.

"It really looks like a road, but . . ." Miike cocked his head and looked about. African snails crawled along on the leaves of the trees. By chance, his eyes fell on a thin, straight object stretching out in both directions—a wire that ran between the trunks of the trees. "A wire?" Miike was wide-eyed with surprise. "Pastor Arakaki! Look at this!"

"I remember now! A wire was strung alongside the road."

"Could it mean . . . ?"

"There's no question. This is where the road was. The one we used to use."

Francisco and Benancio had turned about in surprise.

"Mr. Francisco. The gulch is right over there," Pastor Arakaki continued. "There's a large boulder down in the gulch. There's a cave in the boulder. I want to look for that cave where we did our cooking."

Sure enough, they soon came upon the gulch to the south. The steep slope was overgrown with trees so dense that underbrush couldn't grow in the darkness beneath, and the ground lay damp and bare. They descended, slipping and sliding, grabbing on to trees for support. Bottles, pots, and kettles lay strewn about, evoking the suffering of refugees who had fled the gunfire of war decades ago. Several hundred people had lost their lives in this gulch.

Many large boulders lay along the slope, and it was difficult to find the cave they were searching for. Pastor Arakaki tunneled through the brush searching all around for the cave.

"Here it is! I found it!" They heard Francisco call out. Pastor Arakaki hurried in the direction of his voice.

There, in a boulder shadowed by jungle growth, was a dark tunnel-like hole, a cave.

"Great! Let's go in." The pastor crouched down and entered the cave. Miike followed. Several meters in, rusted water containers, bottles, and canteen lids were strewn about. Many of the water containers and canteen covers were pocked with bullet holes. Pastor Arakaki stared at the scene, and tears glistened in his eyes. "This is it," Pastor Arakaki murmured. He raked the ground with his hand. "Ashes . . ." A frying pan emerged from beneath the ashes. "There's no mistake. This is it. We fried and ate African snails here." The ceiling of the cave was black and sooty.

Pastor Arakaki carried a water container outside. The cameraman shot a close-up of the container. In the cave, it had appeared black, but outside in the sunlight, they could see that the water container had corroded into a rusty brown.

"It's a U.S. military canteen. We picked them up and used them." Pastor Arakaki tapped it lightly with one hand. The brittle canteen crumbled and fell to the ground in pieces. To Miike, the piles of countless white snail shells that covered the ground looked like seashells.

Pastor Arakaki lifted his gaze and said to Francisco. "Thank you. This is the place."

Francisco nodded, and a smile crossed his face.

Pastor Arakaki pointed to the upper slope of the gulch. "On the road up there to the south, about five hundred feet, there was a field of deep, tall grass."

They were near the site of the second murder.

* * * * *

On the night of the first murder, Saburo had been in mental anguish, unable to sleep. Reports that Mr. Asai's body had been discovered threw the Susupe Detention Camp into an uproar.

"Arakaki. You did the right thing. Don't hang your head. Why are you going around with a long face?" MP Jojima asked Saburo.

Jesus Guerrera, former Saipan municipal associate police chief, now hired by civilian American police inspectors, along with the U.S. military police, conducted a careful search for the murder suspect. Mr. Guerrera had a reputation as a master criminal investigator, and he and his subordinates combed the detention camp. Detainees who had had arguments with Mr. Asai or who were viewed with suspicion for some reason were transferred, one after another, to the prison at Chalan Kanoa. Guerrera boasted that he would find the murderer in a week and took on the task with fanatical intensity. Saburo heard rumors that those who denied knowledge of the crime were being tortured.

When Guerrera came around to the #5 barracks, Saburo was among those interrogated. "Do you know who the murderer is?" The piercing eyes behind dark sunglasses glared at him.

Saburo was terrified in his heart, but he answered flatly, "No, I don't know who it is."

"Have you heard any rumors about who the suspect might be?"

"No."

Guerrera wasn't very suspicious of Saburo, who claimed to be a student from the Saipan Vocational School. His two accomplices were not suspected either. This was fortunate, for MP Jojima told them that eight men had been marched to prison on suspicion of being involved.

"Arakaki, tonight, you and I are escaping to the mountains."

"What? What about the people being interrogated?"

"If the actual criminals escape, they'll release the others."

Saburo went along with whatever Jojima said, especially since he believed it would help those who were being falsely accused. He and Jojima escaped successfully and joined Captain Oba and his guerrilla group in Mount Tako. Although liberated from the fear of being imprisoned by

Guerrera, Saburo was never at peace, even when he was alone in the stillness of the jungle. His conscience bothered him. *I killed a human being. But it's not a sin,* he told himself. *It was for the Divine Emperor and the Divine Nation.* But no matter how often he tried to justify what he had done, he couldn't erase the sick feeling in his chest.

Soon he and Jojima heard a report from a volunteer in the detention camp via the farm. According to that source, the escapees "Ryotoku Toma"—the alias Jojima had used in the camp—and Saburo Arakaki were the prime suspects in the murder case. Isamu Sakiyama, who had not been involved in the murder, had been marched to prison. The investigators had interrogated him, thinking he might have some knowledge of the crime, but Sakiyama persistently denied knowing anything. Nonetheless he had apparently been imprisoned at Chalan Kanoa. According to the report, sometime in the near future a man would be sent to the mountain from the farm to lure out the two suspects.

That person was former Japanese soldier Bando (not his real name). He had taken up with an island woman, and it had been discovered that he was living in the civilian detention camp under the guise of being a civilian. However, he didn't want to be separated from the woman, and to avoid this, he was cooperating with the U.S. military. He would be the one to enter the mountains with Jesus Guerrera.

Before long, just as had been reported, a man was seen climbing up the mountain, holding a white flag. Jojima ordered Saburo to wait in hiding while he scouted out the situation. The man met with Captain Oba at Mount Tako. The negotiations continued for almost two weeks.

Jojima returned and announced, "That man is definitely a spy. He says he came to announce that the war is over, but really he is checking out our whereabouts and movements and intends to report it to the U.S. military. If we let him go alive, all fifty of us here will be annihilated. Which is more important—that one man's life or the lives of fifty men? We are fighting for the honor of the Divine Emperor and the Divine Nation."

Saburo found himself unable to disagree with Jojima.

"We'll accompany him part way back down the mountain and then finish him off," Jojima concluded.

Saburo said nothing.

"Arakaki, you come up from behind. When I give you the signal, shoot him." The MP corporal pulled the handgun from his waistband and handed it to Saburo.

* * * * *

When Pastor Arakaki returned to the road above the gulch, he moved to the north through the jungle. Here and there, traces of the old road remained visible. Pastor Arakaki murmured, "We walked along this road. . . ."

Miike followed Pastor Arakaki. After a few hundred feet, the thicket of trees opened onto a field of grass, and they stood beneath the open sky. "Ah. This is the field of grass," Pastor Arakaki blurted out. It was small— only ten meters at most in any direction. The Pastor stopped dead in his tracks. "This is it," he murmured, looking intently at the field. He stood with closed eyes. Silent. Motionless. Miike held his breath and stood beside him.

Francisco and Benancio watched quietly from the thicket, surprise written on their faces. The camera was directed at the pastor's profile.

* * * * *

At the signal to shoot, Saburo pulled the trigger. Bando tumbled into the grass.

"Finish him off," the MP ordered. Saburo coldly shot the man again in the head.

* * * * *

"It was here, the second murder. . . ." Finally, after what seemed like an eternity, the pastor lifted his face. His eyes, when he looked at Miike, were dark and filled with suffering.

"What a horrible crime I committed." Pastor Arakaki clasped his hands together tightly at his chest and closed his eyes in silent prayer. Then he spoke aloud. "Dear God, may his soul rest in peace. Grant those he left behind inner peace."

An indescribable feeling of torment once again overwhelmed Miike. Why had he asked the pastor to go through this experience? He deeply regretted it now.

The pastor's cheeks trembled slightly. "Dear God in heaven, I stand in this very spot once again. I repent of this terrible sin with all my heart and pray that the deceased rest in peace. I stand before You, asking forgiveness. I devote myself to carrying Your gospel in order that such wars will never happen again. I ask for global peace and to save others. I am a weak, sinful man, but You have cleansed me. I ask for the strength to carry out Your work."

Miike stood reverently, his head bowed.

Chapter 12

Surrender and Imprisonment

When the group of forty-eight guerillas under Captain Oba finally surrendered on December 1, 1945, after resisting as long as possible, three and
a half months had already passed since the end of the war. During this
time, the U.S. forces had continued the campaign to wipe out those remaining Japanese soldiers holed up in the mountain who refused to surrender.

One day, Captain Oba's little group heard a Japanese man, claiming to
be Navy Lieutenant Ito, who had been captured in Okinawa, announce
through loudspeakers that Japan had surrendered unconditionally to the
allied forces. Meanwhile, toward the end of November, one of the soldiers
picked up an American magazine, *Life,* in which was a photo of the signing
ceremony of Japan's surrender aboard a U.S. warship. Toward the end of
November, the surviving men gathered at Mount Tako and discussed the
situation. As a result of that meeting, MP Corporal Jojima, acting as the
group's military envoy, descended the mountainside alone. He met with
U.S. Marine Lieutenant-Colonel Howard Kurgis and told him that their
commander would surrender if the American forces would agree to restrict
their access to the mountain and allow memorial services with gun salutes
for those who had died in action on the mountainside. After the surrender,
the group, along with Captain Oba, would be repatriated to Japan. The U.S.
military accepted the Japanese terms. Jojima had bravely volunteered to meet
with the Americans so that the Oba group could surrender with honor.

Saburo's anxiety mounted; he knew that if they surrendered, he might be
imprisoned. One of the conditions of the agreement was that not a single

man be left behind in the mountain. It was decided that Saburo would be incorporated into the force, using the pseudonym, "Private Second Class Tetsuo Yamada."

The group of men who surrendered consisted of thirty from the army and eighteen from the navy—a total of forty-eight people. The weapons in their possession were four army swords, three light machine guns, forty-four small rifles, eight handguns, and eighty-six hand grenades. With clothes, hair clippers, razors, and soap that MP Jojima had secretly acquired through the detention camp, the men were able to clean themselves up. All of them were dressed in military uniforms.

At dawn on December 1, a memorial service for the war dead was held. After a eulogy by Sergeant Fujita, a roll call was taken of the Oba group, and three rifle shots were simultaneously fired skyward. The sound tore through the morning stillness, and the echoes rolled through Mount Tapotchau, where the dead rested.

At 7:30 A.M., the group of forty-eight men under Captain Oba left Mount Tako and marched along the military road. With Sergeant Takase in the lead, carrying the flag of the Rising Sun, they marched toward Garapan. Second Lieutenant Tanabe led the group in singing "The Song of War" as they marched toward an honorable surrender.

Clothed in military uniform, Saburo marched in formation with the soldiers, not knowing what agony awaited him.

* * * * *

With Miike accompanying him, Pastor Arakaki headed toward Matansa Public Elementary School. Beyond the school gate was a long, single-story school building. West of that was a large schoolyard with a growth of Adan trees that continued down to the seashore. It was a weekend, and no students were in sight.

"There was a detention camp here," Pastor Arakaki said. "It was surrounded by triple barbed wire fences, and there were several giant tents set up."

This had once been the spot of the Japanese army's banzai charge. The roar of the sea—or was it the wind?—rumbled through the area. Imura obtained permission to film in the schoolyard.

As the cameras rolled, Pastor Arakaki walked into the schoolyard. Miike asked, "After the surrender, the forty-eight men under Captain Oba came here?"

"Yes, in four trucks."

"Your false identity as Private Tetsuo Yamada wasn't exposed?"

"We were investigated by the American military officials, but somehow I passed. My prisoner of war ID number was around forty-seven hundred or so. I was given an outfit with a POW insignia. I had managed to pass into the camp, but my anxiety didn't subside."

"How many were being held here at that time?"

"A little over three hundred. During the day, we worked outside under the supervision of the U.S. Army."

"You worked?"

"Only for two days after that."

"Only two days?"

"We were pulling weeds in the center of the camp. I saw a jeep carrying an MP enter through the gate. Jesus Guerrera was in the jeep! *This is it,* I thought."

* * * * *

Two MP officers and Investigator Guerrera in dark glasses stepped down from the jeep. The U.S. military guard blew his whistle. "Fall in!"

Saburo instantly thought of running, but soldiers encircled them, their guns cocked. With no choice, he walked toward the center of the grounds. The prisoners were lined up in two rows. Saburo slipped into the middle of the second row.

"We're here to investigate suspects in the Susupe camp murder." A Nisei (second-generation) Japanese-American soldier interpreted.

One by one they were inspected. Inspector Guerrera's fierce eyes gazed into each prisoner's face.

MP Corporal Jojima was the first to be pulled out. "Your rank and name!" the Japanese-American said.

Jojima answered calmly, "Corporal Takeo Jojima." Guerrera glanced at the photo he held in his hand and smiled. The photo of Jojima had been taken for the camp ID card.

Next to be questioned was a superior officer with no connection to the crime.

Finally Jesus Guerrera's huge body stood in front of Saburo. Guerrera's cheeks twitched with laughter, and he snorted. Saburo was resigned to his fate.

"Saburo Arakaki!" Guerrera seized him by his shirtfront.

The three suspects were immediately shoved into the jeep and taken to the police headquarters in Chalan Kanoa.

* * * * *

Now Pastor Arakaki traveled from Matansa, through the town of Garapan, passing Susupe on that very same road toward Chalan Kanoa.

"As you were being transferred by jeep, what was on your mind?" Miike asked.

"I was overcome with anxiety. I whispered to the MP corporal and asked him what we were to do."

"And what did he say?"

"He said to plead ignorance and to persist with that till the end, never admitting that I had killed them."

Miike looked closely at Pastor Arakaki.

"I just nodded," Pastor Arakaki said, looking straight ahead.

In Chalan Kanoa, they traveled back and forth attempting to find the remains of the police headquarters. They asked a number of local residents before they found it—a seemingly ordinary-looking vacant lot, covering an area of no more than 150 meters in any direction.

"I was held prisoner here," Pastor Arakaki said, "as a murderer." His eyes darkened, and he looked toward the sea beyond the trees.

Miike was listening to the low moan of the wind. It sounded as though the land groaned.

Stepping out of the car, Pastor Arakaki looked around. Then he pointed at a tall concrete platform standing between coconut trees. "There was a watch tower on that platform—with an armed guard. There's no doubt;

this is the place. A tall barbed wire fence surrounded it. Regular criminals were being held here."

Miike entered the vacant lot. In the area that grass hadn't overgrown lay a concrete floor. He found a rusted water faucet.

"The old shower room," Pastor Arakaki murmured. He walked around investigating the lot and stood on a corner of concrete. "I was in a solitary confinement cell about here."

* * * * *

Two Quonset huts stood in a row at the prison. At the gate in the southwest corner was the police box of the military and local police. The three prisoners were taken to separate solitary confinement cells.

Saburo was the first to be dragged into the interrogation room.

Inspector Jesus Guerrera sat in a chair; he offered Saburo a cigarette with a smile.

"How's it going, Saburo?"

I will not be taken in by his tricks, Saburo told himself.

"You hungry?" The question was asked kindly, but the eyes behind the sunglasses were strangely eerie.

"We know that the murders in the Susupe camp and in the mountain were your doings—you and Jojima. I want you to tell me about it in detail, truthfully."

Saburo answered unflinchingly, "I know nothing of the incidents."

"What? You liar!"

"I'm innocent."

"So you're going to try to fool me, are you? Don't think you can get away with it!" Anger surfaced in Guerrera's dark face. Saburo sealed his lips.

"Are you going to pretend you're innocent?" Guerrera stood up.

"If I don't know, I don't know. I am Tetsuo Yamada, private in . . ." Before he could finish, Guerrera slapped him hard in the face.

Saburo gritted his teeth. Jojima had said to persist by pretending not to know anything.

At Guerrera's signal, two young men entered the room and stood in front of Saburo. They were Vicente Sablan and Juan Blanco, both students two years ahead of Saburo at the Saipan Vocational School. He knew both of them.

"Saburo, give up." The two young men glared at him with cold eyes.

Guerrera burst into angry shouts. "Confess, Arakaki!"

"I know nothing!" he shouted.

"Get him!" Guerrera spoke, and instantly his subordinates leaped onto Saburo. Clenched fists slammed his jaw. Feet kicked him in the groin. The intense pain enraged Saburo, and he rushed toward his attackers in a fury. He threw one over his shoulder, but the punching and kicking continued until he eventually collapsed in defeat. When his consciousness returned, he was lying on the cot in his solitary cell.

That evening, Saburo was once again dragged out of his cell and into the interrogation chambers.

"Saburo! Are you going to keep on lying? You want to hurt really bad?" Jesus Guerrera grilled him with a menacing look.

The unmitigated pain in his body fed Saburo's anger. He held his tongue obstinately.

"All right. If you're going to keep your mouth shut, I've got something for you." Guerrera said. "I'll do it like the Japanese military police would do it."

His subordinates bound Saburo's hands and feet with rope, dragged him to the kitchen, and laid him face up on a large table. Clenching a hose attached to the faucet, one of the men stood over Saburo and said, "Well, are you going to confess or not? What we do depends on your answer."

Saburo said nothing. He would never confess. He was sticking to what Jojima had told him to do.

"He's a stubborn one. Give him a drink," Guerrera ordered.

Water poured from the hose. The subordinate forced the hose into Saburo's mouth. Immediately his mouth filled with water, and he couldn't breathe. A splitting pain rushed into his head. He kept swallowing the water. He shook his head desperately, but hands held his head down. The water that spilled from his mouth filled his eyes. Everything began to grow fuzzy. His stomach hurt. He couldn't breathe.

I'm going to die, he thought. In desperation, he threw up both legs, tied together, and kicked the burly man holding the hose in the crotch. The man fell head over heels and rolled onto the floor.

"Give him some more!" Guerrera snarled, and the men descended on Saburo with clubs. Blood spurted from between his eyebrows. His breathing came with increasing difficulty, and his consciousness was slowly slipping away.

When he came to later on the cot in his cell, Saburo moaned in agonizing pain.

"What happened? Are you OK, Arakaki?" Jojima whispered from the next cell. Saburo couldn't answer. Tears of pain and frustration flowed from his eyes, and suppressing all sounds, he cried silently.

Chapter 13

Torture and Confession

The questioning continued the following day.

"Confess! What happened to the weapon?" Jesus Guerrera persisted. Saburo stubbornly held his tongue, desperately enduring the interrogation.

"So, Saburo, who told you to do it?" Guerrera suddenly changed his line of questioning and spoke in a softer tone. "I can't imagine that a student from the Saipan Vocational School would come up with a scheme like this and carry it out all by himself. Who told you to do it? If you answer honestly, your crime will be lighter. Think carefully."

Saburo closed his eyes and held his breath. He was overcome with terror that if he let even one word slip from his mouth, the rest would come pouring out.

"It's painful, isn't it? It'll be easier if you talk. Who told you to do it?" A smile lurked on Guerrera's lips as he looked at Saburo's face distorted in agony. "Come on now, cough it up, Saburo. It won't hurt you."

Saburo was struggling within. *Why must I face this kind of suffering? Is this for the Divine Emperor? For the Divine Nation?* Saburo's angry thoughts were tangled up in his mind.

"Saburo, do you want to drink water again?" Guerrera asked lightly. Saburo couldn't stop the trembling that began to ripple through his body.

"Confess!" Guerrera stood up impatiently and screamed at him. Saburo jumped to his feet and cursed Guerrera. The guards leaped on him immediately, pinning him to the ground. Then they dragged him once again into the kitchen and subjected him to the brutal water torture. He couldn't breathe, and he was sure he would die.

It would be better if I were dead. The thought flashed through his mind.

"So, you feel like talking now, Saburo?"

I don't care what you do to me anymore. He was in agony and struggling to breathe.

"Confess or you'll keep drinking water. Do you want to die?"

A fury burst into flame in Saburo's chest. "Go ahead! Kill me, if you can! Kill me!" he screamed out in a mad rage.

Guerrera's face turned red, and he slugged Saburo. Then he motioned to his guards, who jumped in, kicking and beating the prisoner violently.

This is it. I'm going to be killed, Saburo thought just before he passed out from the pain.

His back throbbed. A fiery pain pierced his forehead. Shells fired from warships exploded all around. Bomb blasts pounded into the ground. He had fallen on the very edge of jagged cliffs. *Oh, this is the cliff at Marpi.* Shells flew in from the sea, shrieking in the air. A young girl with a bobbed haircut, dressed in a blue T-shirt, was lying on a rock shelf. She got lightly to her feet. *That's dangerous,* Saburo thought.

The girl slowly turned around. Shining black eyes. He had seen them somewhere. His mother's eyes! A pure smile surfaced on her face. She suddenly looked older. *My mother—when she was a girl?* He was about to call out to her in a loud voice when there was an explosion. The young girl had vanished. *Where did you go? Mama, where did you go!* Tears poured from his eyes. He was so sad, he sobbed.

"Arakaki! Can you hear me? Arakaki . . ." The muffled voice brought him back to himself. He had been dreaming. Tears were streaming down his face, and he had been crying out. The pain that wracked his body pushed him roughly back into reality. He found himself lying on his cot in the solitary cell.

"Arakaki! Are you OK?" The voice was coming from the cell next door.

"Do you know who this is? It's Jojima," the corporal lowered his voice and whispered. Saburo couldn't see his face.

Under orders from Jojima, Saburo had murdered two people. And he had been told to never speak of it. Following those instructions, he had undergone terrible torture until he was half dead, half alive.

"Arakaki, you're doing a good job. You're hurting badly, I know. I'm sorry." At the unexpected kind words, Saburo's emotions burst forth—one sob, and then a torrent that he could not stifle.

"You're not the only one going through terrible questioning. I am, too," Jojima whispered.

Saburo was silent. Overwhelmed with emotions, he found himself unable to speak.

"Arakaki, can you hear me?"

"Yes."

"Would you be willing to die with me?"

"What!" Saburo doubted his ears for a moment.

Jojima continued in a low voice, "I'm ashamed even for surrendering; it's a terrible disgrace. Instead of being tortured in the questioning, I think I'll choose death."

Saburo was shocked. He was at the brink of utter despair, and he, too, had thought it might be better to die.

"What about you? Are you willing to die?" Jojima asked again.

Saburo did not hesitate. "If it would be with you, I'd die happily," he replied to the tempting suggestion.

"Is that how you feel? Thank you. . . ."

"But how will we die?" Saburo asked. The answer didn't come back immediately. Perhaps the corporal was thinking for a while. There was a pause, and then he spoke with persuasion. "This is what we'll do, Saburo. Let's both confess what we did. I'm being questioned about killing U.S. prisoners, spying, and obstructing those who were trying to surrender. I don't think I can get out of it. There's no doubt—it's a death sentence."

Saburo listened.

"Arakaki. You tell them that you committed the two murders by yourself. You're the one who killed them. Say that you did it of your own will. If you do that, you and I, we can die together." This was not like any orders Saburo had received before, but there was something about it that kept him from saying no.

"Admit that I committed the murders? By myself?"

"Yes. And that no one ordered you to do so. That you did it purely out of loyalty to Japan."

It was true that he had carried out the operation believing it was for the emperor and Japan.

"I . . . I understand. . . ." Saburo decided he would confess.

* * * * *

"You completely believed the corporal, didn't you?" Miike asked.

Pastor Arakaki gazed into the sky and nodded slowly, his face solemn. "I was nineteen years old. I trusted that man from the bottom of my heart. I admired his judgment. He seemed to always make the right decisions. On Mount Tapotchau, we escaped death several times due to his directions. I thought for sure that if death should strike, it would be together with him. We would die together."

Miike listened intently. But something else ran through his mind. The corporal must have realized that if the torture continued, Saburo would eventually crack and spill the whole story, confessing the crime and implicating the others too—that would have messed up his plan.

Pastor Arakaki stood silently where the solitary cell had been. In the cracked concrete floor underfoot, wild grass had set down its roots. Here on this floor of the solitary cell, a young, naive boy had sat in isolation, not knowing to question anything.

* * * * *

The next day, Saburo was again dragged from the solitary cell to the interrogation room. Before the questioning could begin, Saburo blurted out, "I will tell you the truth about what happened."

A surprised Jesus Guerrero looked closely at Saburo.

Saburo had not slept well the previous night; he had kept picturing himself being executed by a firing squad. He had concluded that the only way that he would be able to keep his sanity would be to spit out the whole story, like throwing himself off a cliff.

"I did it. I killed them both," Saburo burst out.

"What made you decide to admit it?" Guerrero said with a chilling smile.

Saburo closed his eyes.

"Under whose order did you do it?"

Saburo did not respond.

"Who ordered you to do it?"

"No one."

"Who did it with you?"

"I did it by myself."

"What did you do with the murder weapon?"

"I left it in the camp. In the number seven section public lavatory."

"At least that much is the truth," Guerrero broke into a sarcastic grin. The U.S. Army bayonet was found in the public lavatory in Susupe Camp, just as Saburo had confessed. The weapon that had been used in the killing of the former Japanese soldier—a U.S. Colt .45 caliber revolver—had been among the weapons handed over during the formal surrender ceremony of Captain Oba's unit.

The commissioned officer who received Jesus Guerrero's report arrived early the next day accompanied by a Nisei interpreter. Saburo was taken by jeep to the weapons arsenal near Donnay.

"Which of these handguns did you use?" The officer inquired, showing him eight handguns. Three were similar to the one that had been used in the murder.

"I'm not sure." Saburo's statement triggered a troubled look on the officer's face.

"Oh, well. Just pick one," the officer said. Saburo had no choice. He picked out one of the handguns. He didn't really care anymore what happened.

Chapter 14

Sentenced to Death!

A U.S. Naval Legal Affairs officer came to take a deposition from Saburo that detailed the crime. Repeatedly, he grilled Saburo regarding whether he had actually acted alone. Saburo insisted that he had. He was determined he would not admit to having accomplices.

Although Saburo wasn't aware of it, MP Corporal Jojima was no longer at Chalan Kanoa Prison. "Mr. Jojima . . . Mr. Jojima . . . ," he called out repeatedly, but there was no response from the next cell. When he finally asked one of the guards, Saburo found out that Jojima had been returned to the POW camp at Matansa.

In March of the following year, the criminal trial for the two murders convened in Susupe. Saburo was escorted from prison by jeep to stand trial at the Naval and Military Court Martial in a special courtroom that had been set up within the civilian government facilities.

A navy captain presided on the judge's bench. The American flag and the navy flag flew proudly in the courtroom. Flanking the courtroom on both sides was the jury—about ten military officers. The defendant was represented by Lieutenant Commander Fink and two civilian attorneys.

The presiding judge called the court to order.

"Do you swear that all the testimony you will give in this court will be the truth, the whole truth, and nothing but the truth, so help you God?" The question was difficult to understand due to the awkward translation by the Nisei military interpreter, but Saburo responded with a "Yes."

The charge was first-degree murder, and the trial proceeded at a brisk pace. Prosecution read the indictment. Saburo sat stiffly in the defendant's chair, not fully comprehending the nature of the charges against him.

On the second day of the trial, a middle-aged Japanese man with a strained expression on his face took the witness stand. He identified himself as Isamu Yaka, an instructor at the National School. Yaka was sworn in as a defense witness. The defense attorney, Lieutenant Commander Fink, began his examination of the witness. "I ask the witness—did the defendant receive a military education?"

"Yes. Military training was conducted in all of the middle schools. As a student at the Saipan Vocational School, the defendant would have received training to fight in defense of the country."

"Can you tell us how many hours a week would have been allotted for military education?"

"I wouldn't know exactly."

"In Japan, do they teach that military orders are direct orders from the emperor?"

"That is what is taught."

"In Japan, would anyone who spoke disparaging, disrespectful words about the emperor be sentenced to death?"

"Just saying disrespectful words would not bring on the death penalty. However, if I remember correctly, there is a provision in the penal code that says that anyone who kills or attempts to kill the emperor would be sentenced to death."

"I ask the witness, in the schools in Japan, do they teach that the emperor is a god?"

"Yes, that is what is taught."

"Is the emperor a god even though Japan met with defeat in war?"

"I cannot answer that question."

The significance and purpose of the questioning did not make any sense to Saburo.

When the second witness entered the courtroom, Saburo was taken aback and almost stood to his feet. It was his classmate, Isamu Sakiyama. He appeared so thin and haggard that for a moment Saburo doubted his eyes.

Jesus Guerrero had interrogated Sakiyama after Saburo and MP Corporal Jojima had escaped from Susupe Camp to the mountains. Sakiyama had maintained that he had no knowledge about, nor any relationship to, the incidents. He was then, apparently, held at Chalan Kanoa Prison. Sakiyama must have received severe torture during his interrogation.

Because Sakiyama had been performing simple chores in the U.S. Military Office, Jojima had removed him from the assassination team. Thus Sakiyama had not participated in the murder of Mr. Asai. Even so, he was subjected to intense grilling and when threatened with torture, he submitted readily. What were his feelings toward Saburo?

Saburo started to rise, but the MP guard grabbed him by the shoulders and forced him to sit back down.

Sakiyama took his oath at the witness stand. Lieutenant Commander Fink commenced with the examination.

"Do you know the defendant?"

"Yes."

"Did you and the defendant receive the same education?"

"Yes. He's my classmate. We were classmates at the Saipan Vocational School."

"I ask the witness, do you consider it good to die for the sake of the emperor?"

Sakiyama was silent for a moment. "They taught us that a true Japanese should willingly give up his life for the emperor—for Japan."

"Do you believe the defendant would lie?"

Sakiyama glanced at Saburo. He couldn't detect any trace of resentment in his eyes, and he looked visibly sorrowful.

"Saburo is . . . I believe Saburo Arakaki is an honest man."

"Tell me more about the defendant's character."

"Saburo is the type of guy who sticks up for the weak. I saw him once helping a classmate—a younger classmate who was wounded—even at the risk of his own life." Saburo looked intently at Sakiyama.

"Do you think the defendant murdered the victims?"

"I can't imagine that Saburo could kill anyone."

Saburo felt his eyes grow suddenly warm and moist.

As Sakiyama completed his testimony and left the courtroom, he glanced at Saburo sitting in the defendant's box. *Hang in there,* his eyes said.

Thank you, Saburo answered with the look in his eyes.

The trial concluded after only five days. The verdict: guilty. The sentence: the death penalty.

* * * * *

Palm leaves rustled in the wind.

"I had resigned myself to what might happen, but when I actually heard the death sentence pronounced, I felt a chill rush through my body as if the blood had drained from my head. I could barely stand." Pastor Arakaki closed his eyes. He stood for a long time in the torrid sunshine, before the remains of the cell where he had been kept in solitary confinement. He was silent, but his inner pain was evident.

Miike did not know what to say. Something within his own heart bothered him. *Why did I bring him here?* Ever since they had visited the two murder sites, this thought had haunted him.

Pastor Arakaki sat down on the concrete floor. A large black ant climbed up his leg. For a while he followed the movement of the ant with his eyes. Miike sat next to him. The nineteen-year-old Saburo had once sat here as a convict on death row. Sitting there in the bright sunlight, Miike could not picture it. He closed his eyes. But he still simply could not visualize the scene—Saburo, a nineteen-year-old convict on death row.

"Mr. Miike. When you hear the death sentence handed down, you feel a desperate desire to cling to life. I thought of escaping. But . . . " Pastor Arakaki pointed to the concrete foundation where the watchtower once stood. "Looking out the window of my solitary cell, I could see a watchtower just outside. Armed guards stood there twenty-four hours a day, constantly watching. At the southeast corner was a gate. Every time a jeep came through that gate with an MP aboard, I thought for sure that it had come to take me to my execution."

Miike nodded.

"The sound of the changing of the guards, the sound of their boots, the sound of their rifles during rifle inspection terrified me. I desperately wanted to live, but at the same time I also felt that it would be better to die quickly. I thought that death was inevitable and that if I was to die it would be together with Jojima, facing a firing squad, so I wanted to die. There was an older Chamorro guard there that I used to see all the time. One day when he brought my meal, I asked him if he knew what had happened to Jojima, the MP corporal."

"What did he say?"

"That Jojima had been declared innocent."

Miike was stunned and didn't know what to say.

"I shouted at him, 'What? Innocent! Are you sure? What happened?' "

"The Chamorro guard shook his head. He didn't know, except that Jojima had been returned to the Matansa POW camp."

Miike listened.

"I had been deceived. For the first time I realized that I had been completely betrayed." Pastor Arakaki suddenly opened his eyes and stood. "I was burning with anger. I cursed. I remember vowing to never forget and to take revenge! I would kill Jojima!"

"I think I can understand. . . ," Miike began.

"But there was absolutely nothing I could do," Pastor Arakaki went on. "I appealed to the court, telling the authorities that I had committed the crime in obedience to an order by an MP. But it was too late. Eventually, I couldn't even eat. I couldn't bring myself to swallow my food."

Miike rose to his feet, his eyes never leaving Pastor Arakaki. The pastor rose as well and stepped forward, wild grass crumpling beneath his feet. Then he stopped in his tracks. He gazed into the sky and spoke. "Later, I heard that the Matansa POW camp had been closed down. All of the Japanese POWs were shipped back to Japan by boat. The Susupe camp was burned down. Here I was left alone. Would I be executed today? Tomorrow? Almost every night I had nightmares of the moment just before being shot to death. Constantly tormented by the fear of dying, I soon became emaciated like a skeleton. Day after day I cried out, screaming like a mad man."

Miike looked heavenward and took in a deep breath. The blue sky stretched on endlessly, bathed in bright sunlight. *Why had heaven cornered this honest, simple young boy in the valley of death?*

"One day, a commissioned officer arrived with an interpreter. I was sure the day of my execution had arrived. The officer read from the paper he held in his hand. It said that I would be transferred to Guam the next day." Pastor Arakaki was silent for a long while. Then he continued, "Death sentence executions took place in Guam. The next day I was escorted under heavy security to be shipped out to Guam by troop transport ship from Garapan Harbor."

On a ship rocked gently by the swelling ocean of the Marianas, Saburo had been transported overnight to Guam, where the execution chamber awaited him.

On a Boeing 727 the flight time from Saipan to Guam is thirty-five minutes. Pastor Arakaki, Miike, and the rest of the entourage headed from Guam International Airport to Agana, driving along the shoreline Marine Drive, Highway 1, lined by rows of palm trees and white coral sands. Agana, the capital of Guam, is located about midpoint of the stretch of beach on the western shore. It is a town surrounded by thick green tropical trees.

A pure white structure, the Dolce Nombre de Maria Cathedral Basilica, stood within the perimeter of the plaza, with its expansive green lawns. Here too, Japanese tour groups strolled conspicuously along this popular tourist spot.

Research among the historical documents at the nearby library resulted in the discovery that following the Pacific War, the Japanese War Crimes Prison had stood just outside the current plaza. Today, the police department building stands in that spot. Pastor Arakaki climbed out of the vehicle and stood for a long moment in the middle of the large police department parking lot. "It's all so changed," he murmured. There was nothing to indicate that a prison had ever stood there.

Pastor Arakaki looked around. A certain spot toward the east—a hilly region surrounded by green foliage—caught his eye.

"You know, I sort of remember the shape of that hill. I also remember that directly west of here was the ocean. This must be the place where I was brought to be executed."

* * * * *

Saburo was surprised. Compared to the prison in Saipan, the one in Guam was much more elaborate. Three layers of barbed wire fenced off the entire area. More than a dozen long Quonset buildings, lined with prison cells, stood in parallel rows. Guard towers, manned by sentries armed with machine guns, were positioned at the four corners of the prison. A single glance was enough to reveal the level of strict control.

The cellblock was divided into two sections—one for death row criminals and another for convicts serving defined terms. To ward off the swarming mosquitoes, prisoners rubbed mosquito repellent into their skin from head to toe. To prevent escapes, powerful lights illuminated the entire cellblock with a brightness that made night seem almost like the daytime. Each convict on death row was assigned a Marine guard, who kept a vigilant eye on the prisoner under his surveillance. Once again, Saburo was placed by himself in a small cell. To prevent suicide attempts, he was stripped to the waist and given only a pair of shorts to wear.

The food was dreadful. The U.S. military cook prepared rice, but it was too soft and tasted awful to the Japanese palate. A stew of sorts, made from military field rations of boiled potatoes and beef, was poured over the rice.

But perhaps most agonizing and humiliating for the prisoners was having to use the toilet located in the center of the prison yard. Prisoners had no choice but to relieve themselves in complete view of the guard. One's former rank had no bearing on the treatment received; whether one had been a common soldier, junior officer, or command-level senior officer, the guards were equally rough on all and seemed to have no qualms about ridiculing and verbally abusing the prisoners. Saburo's deep-seated anti-American sentiments grew even stronger. *American pigs!* he cursed them in his heart.

Perhaps they sensed the hatred in his eyes. The guards often glared at him or screamed insults in words that he couldn't understand. Saburo shook his head; he did not understand. This seemed only to egg them on. They responded with exaggerated gestures, encircling their necks with both hands, cruelly mimicking Saburo being hung.

You've got it wrong; I'm going to be shot by a firing squad, right? he thought, inadvertently letting them see the bewilderment on his face. The guards roared with laughter. Still Saburo was sure that he would be executed by a firing squad. He lived from day to day in a constant struggle against fear, with no idea when his death sentence would be meted out—whether today or perhaps tomorrow.

The Japanese prisoners were strictly prohibited from speaking to each other—not even a simple greeting to the prisoner in the next cell. So there was no way to know for sure what went on in the cell next door. But Saburo kept an eye on all movement in the death row cells directly across from his. The prison chaplain, an elderly priest dressed in a black robe and wearing wooden clogs, visited the cells. Saburo noticed that after three visits by the priest, a death row convict did not return to his cell. The following morning the door of the cell would be left swinging open. No doubt, that convict's execution day had arrived.

There were no unusual sounds, no gunshots from a firing squad. It seemed that the executions took place somewhere outside the prison. The *clop, clop, clop* of the priest's clogs would be heard, and a few days later, from some cell somewhere in the block, a convict would disappear, never to return. Who would it be tonight?

His inevitable fate approached.

I don't want to die! I don't want to be killed! The thoughts tore at Saburo's throat. He wanted to scream. Thinking about it only drove him closer to madness. He cursed Jojima who had betrayed him and plunged him into this hell. *Even if I die, I will torment him and will kill him.* Vengeance burned uncontrollably in his heart. Despair, fury, and the horror of death harassed him constantly.

At night Saburo stretched out on his wooden board to sleep, but sleep brought only a recurring nightmare of being chased and cornered in the fierce mopping-up operation on Mount Tapotchau—and then being shot. He awoke, screaming.

The sleepless nights continued; the days were hot and draining. Saburo was confined to the tiny cell, and there was absolutely nothing to do. One day as he sat cross-legged on the cell floor, aimless, blank-minded, he noticed a black ant that had somehow entered the cell. He extended a finger to the creature, and the ant crawled onto his hand. Saburo stared at the ant creeping along his palm. The lively antennae on its head, the roving black eyeballs, the ant's movements were interesting to watch. Watching the tiny insect brought back memories of Okinawa and his childhood. *I wonder how my younger sisters are doing. Grandmother . . . and Mother,* he mused. The image of his busy father, constantly working, seemed to be reflected in this black ant that moved busily about. As he thought about never seeing any of his loved ones again, his eyes filled with tears. *I guess there is nothing to do but to resign myself to my fate and give up,* he thought.

One day, a white bird flew over the shoulder of his guard and into Saburo's cell. A free-flying bird! How he envied it. *Oh, to be a bird! To be free!*

As Saburo watched, the bird flew out and landed on the roof. Suddenly he noticed that in the death-row cellblock across from his own, a guard was tossing some sort of cardboard package into each cell. *I wonder what it is?* It was a fairly small rectangular box. *Chocolate?* Sometimes the prisoners were granted a piece of moldy chocolate after meals. *This must be something special.*

Saburo waited anxiously for the guard to come to his cell. *Thump!* No sooner had the package hit the floor than he quickly began tearing off the wrapping. It was a thick book. On the cover were the Japanese words, "The New Testament of the Bible. The New Testament of our Savior and Lord Jesus Christ. New York, London, Tokyo, Christian Bible Society."

Then in English, the letters "U. S. A." The book must have been published in America. *Oh, so this is Christian stuff!* Saburo snorted. In his native village in Okinawa, Christianity was detested because it was a Westerner's religion.

Saburo had never before come into contact with this book called the Bible. The pages within were written in Japanese. His eyes were hungry for the chance to read something in Japanese. And he had nothing else to do. So he opened to the first page and began to read: "The Gospel of Matthew. Chapter 1. The book of genealogy of Jesus Christ, the Son of David, the Son of Abraham: Abraham begot Isaac, Isaac begot Jacob, and Jacob begot

Judah and his brothers. Judah begot Perez and Zerah by Tamar, Perez begot Hezron, and . . ."

The uninteresting sentences continued on and on. What is this anyway? Saburo asked himself. The language made little sense to him; it was almost incomprehensible. He tossed the book to the floor and stretched himself out next to it. Then a thought came to him: *Hey, this could be handy.* He picked up the Bible and tried it out as a pillow. It was sure better than no pillow at all. From that day he prized his new pillow. But, he never thought, not even once, of opening its pages again.

The prison chaplain offered to visit him, but Saburo refused outright. He wanted nothing to do with religion, whether Buddhist or Christian.

Clop, clop, clop . . . the sound of wooden clogs could be heard in the distance. Saburo followed the sound of the clogs daily to guess which prison cell the priest was visiting. Reclining in his cell, head on his "pillow," Saburo listened to the sound approaching, closer and closer. It must be for someone in this cellblock. He raised himself up and listened closely. *Clop, clop, clop.* The sound continued to draw nearer. Saburo got to his feet, heart suddenly beating faster. Now he could see the black robe. The priest stopped directly in front of Saburo's cell. Saburo held his breath.

"Good afternoon." The priest peered over the iron bars of the cell; he wore black-rimmed eyeglasses. Saburo's mind went blank. A guard was closely watching from the side. "How are you doing? Is everything all right?" The priest asked, his gaze stony.

Saburo's body froze; he couldn't find his voice. The priest noticed and spoke more kindly. "Please, get a hold of yourself."

Saburo remained silent.

"Take courage, Suzuki-san."

"What?"

"Let's just take our time and talk it out."

"Wait! You're mistaken! I'm Arakaki!"

"What?" It was the priest's turn to be surprised. The guard nodded his head, indicating that the prisoner was indeed Arakaki.

"Oh, sorry! It was a mistake. A mistake. Sorry, sorry." The priest laughed wryly.

But Saburo couldn't find it in himself to smile. He melted to the floor, his energy drained.

The days of despair and the constant fear of not being able to see a tomorrow continued for about a year. Then in early July 1947, two guards, accompanied by a Japanese-American translator, suddenly stood in front of Saburo's cell. "Saburo Arakaki, you are to report to the warden's office immediately. We will accompany you there."

Two guards held Saburo on either side as he was half-carried, half-walked, toward the warden's office. He had no strength to resist. All he could imagine was that the date of his execution had been set and was going to be disclosed to him.

He entered the chief warden's office. An American flag stood in one corner of the office. The warden was dressed in a navy uniform. A tense Saburo stood at attention before him.

"Are you Saburo Arakaki?"

"Yes!" A measure of composure returned. *Whatever I am told, Saburo thought, I will stand tall. I am a Japanese, and this is the final expression of pride.*

The chief warden stood up; for some reason he had a faint smile on his face. He began reading from the documents in his hands as the Nisei interpreter translated for Saburo.

"Regarding your case of murder on the island of Saipan, as a result of a rehearing in Washington, D.C., by the Justice Department, after consideration of the circumstances, the first class crime has been reduced, and the sentence has been reduced to life imprisonment. The serving of your time will . . ."

Saburo heard nothing else the warden said. The instant the words life imprisonment penetrated his consciousness, it was as if he had awakened from a nightmare and a light had been turned on. *I escaped the death sentence!* Fear instantly vanished from his heart, and a well of joy sprang up in its place. *I won't be killed! I will be able to live!*

He was overwhelmed with joy, and warm tears filled his eyes. With his heart quivering with happiness, Saburo returned to his solitary cell.

A few days later he was again called to the warden's office.

"Saburo Arakaki. You will be sent to Hawaii to serve your life imprisonment," the warden told him.

"Why Hawaii? I killed a Japanese. Let me serve out my sentence in Japan!" Saburo entreated.

"No!"

"Why? Why does it have to be Hawaii?"

"I don't know. It's a decision that came from Washington, D.C."

"There must be something wrong with this! Please ask why I have to serve my sentence in Hawaii."

"There isn't time. On July 15, you will board a transport ship for Honolulu."

"I don't want to go to Hawaii! Please, I beg of you!"

"This is a command! I cannot change it."

Saburo's joy at being spared the death sentence seemed short lived. Why did he have to be taken even farther away from Japan, to a territory of the United States, a country he knew nothing of? And to Hawaii of all places? To think that he would now have to spend the rest of his life serving a life sentence in enemy territory was more than he could accept. He ardently pleaded to serve his sentence in Japan—but to no avail.

On the evening of July 15, Saburo was dragged from his solitary cell, even as he violently protested being sent to Hawaii. He vehemently poured out his discontent on the warden who warned him to quietly submit to all orders. He was handcuffed and forced into a jeep. Two armed guards in military uniform were under orders to transfer the convict to Hawaii. The jeep started toward the military pier. Saburo continued to loudly express his discontentment and complaints. In the western horizon, the large sun began its passage down into the ocean.

* * * * *

"I just couldn't understand why I was being sent to Hawaii." Pausing on the white sands of the beach, Pastor Arakaki spoke softly, looking out over the sea. "I strongly fought and resisted even at the military pier. I had to be put on the ship by sheer force."

"Have you ever thought about what would have happened if you had been sent back to Japan instead?" Miike asked. Looking at the profile of Pastor Arakaki's face, illuminated by the sun on the western horizon, he detected a faint smile.

"I don't know what would have happened. But my companion in Saipan, a classmate from school there, Isamu Sakiyama, said that if I had not become a Christian, I may have become a boss in organized crime, a gangster, or perhaps even a menace to society," the pastor laughed brightly.

After the sun set, the emerald green of the ocean quickly faded and darkened. As the last vestiges of light died, Pastor Arakaki said, "In the night, the boat left the port and headed toward Hawaii. My happiness upon receiving the reduced sentence had been totally transformed into a deep despair."

Miike, too, wondered why Saburo had been sent to Hawaii. Back then, there were reportedly about four hundred convicted and suspected war criminals being held in the prison at Guam. War crimes in the Central Pacific Region, such as the murder of POWs on Truk Island, were brought to trial in Guam, at the U.S. Naval Military Court, where many of those who received the death penalty were executed. The last execution to be performed there was in March 1950, nearly five years after the end of the war. Of those who had received sentences of definite terms of imprisonment, many were sent to Sugamo Prison in Tokyo to serve out their remaining time. It seemed that perhaps Saburo Arakaki was the only prisoner who had been sent from Guam to Hawaii to serve out his sentence.

As they walked along the sand beach, Pastor Arakaki said, "The reason I was sent to Hawaii came to me only after many years."

Tomorrow, they would head to Hawaii.

Chapter 15

Prisoner J-608

Crossing the International Date Line, Pastor Arakaki, Miike, and the film crew continued their trip across the Pacific Ocean to Hawaii, a little over three thousand miles (five thousand kilometers) from Guam. It was barely daybreak when they arrived. Pastor Kojiro Matsunami of the Honolulu Japanese Seventh-day Adventist Church met the group at the airport. He appeared to be in his forties and had kind eyes.

"Welcome, Pastor Arakaki. We've gotten permission from Oahu Prison to visit the facility. They have agreed to let us see the solitary confinement cells also."

"We are grateful for that. Thank you very much for your efforts, Pastor Matsunami." Pastor Arakaki's large hands firmly grasped and shook the slender hands of Pastor Matsunami. Miike had very much doubted that Pastor Arakaki would be permitted to see the cell where he had spent his sentence. Pastor Matsunami and the elders of the church must have made special efforts to obtain permission.

"Thank you so much for all of the trouble you must have gone through," Miike said.

"I want you to be able to do a good job," said Pastor Matsunami, smiling warmly.

After they had loaded their bags and camera equipment into the church car, the lanky Pastor Matsunami folded his tall body into the driver's seat. "Before we start," he said and closed his eyes and clasped his hands together. "In the precious name of the Lord Jesus Christ, I offer my grateful prayer. Please pour out heaven's abundant blessings on the work of Pastor Arakaki. And I pray that

You will provide Your guiding hand over this documentary film project and that the crew will be able to carry out their work smoothly. . . ."

Pastor Arakaki's thoughts went back forty years.

* * * * *

Ten days after the transport ship left Guam, Saburo landed at Pearl Harbor on the island of Oahu in Hawaii. He had been violently seasick as the ship rocked wildly back and forth in the huge waves of the Pacific. He arrived in Hawaii looking haggard and emaciated.

Still he looked around with interest at Pearl Harbor, where the war in the Pacific theater had been ignited by the Japanese surprise attack on December 7, 1941. It had been a shocking blow to the U.S. Pacific Fleet. President Roosevelt, standing before Congress, bitterly criticized this "day of infamy" and declared war on Japan.

The day he arrived, however, the sky was clear and peaceful; Pearl Harbor was bathed with warm blue waters that drifted gently in the harbor. Yet Saburo sensed a hostile anti-Japanese sentiment that seemed to pervade the harbor's atmosphere. For him, Hawaii was the worst possible place he could have been taken. Wherever he turned, he met foreign faces and words he could not understand. To think of spending the rest of his life confined to a dungeon, all alone, not knowing a single person, in this foreign land reeking with enmity was almost more than he could bear. His feet grew heavy with despair as he stepped off the ship.

Saburo was temporarily locked up in a U.S. Navy holding cell at the harbor. The next day, he was transported by jeep to the Oahu Prison facility in Honolulu.

After undergoing a thorough physical examination, being photographed, and signing legal papers, Saburo Arakaki, sentenced to life imprisonment, was thrown into a solitary confinement cell on the third floor of the prison's cellblock. He was twenty-one years old.

* * * * *

Today, Oahu Prison is known as the State of Hawaii Oahu Correctional Center. The facility is located west of downtown Honolulu in the district of Kalihi. A short distance south is Keehi Lagoon. To the east is Sand Island, where many Japanese Americans from Hawaii were detained after the outbreak of the Pacific war. Japanese military prisoners of war, apprehended in the Pacific, were also confined there. After the war, these POWs were returned to Japan.

Saburo, who had been sentenced in a U.S. general military court martial in the Marianas, was under the jurisdiction of the U.S. Navy. With a reduced sentence of life imprisonment, he had been transferred to Oahu Prison to serve his prison term.

The star spangled banner fluttered in the wind from its position atop a tall pole at the new entrance on the west side of the correctional facility. Toward the back and to the left of the compound stood an old gray building. Pastor Arakaki pointed. "That is where I was held."

"In a solitary confinement cell?" asked Miike.

"Yes, and in the mixed group cells too."

"You came just in time," Pastor Matsunami commented. "That building, I understand, is going to be torn down this year."

At the reception office, the group was required to sign documents for permission to enter the prison. "Chief Warden Shimada will meet with you," announced the Japanese-American woman who guided them into the reception room.

Warden Takeo Shimada, also a Japanese-American, dressed in a dark blue aloha shirt, entered the room and greeted them. He shook hands with Pastor Arakaki. "Welcome, Mr. Arakaki. I've heard about you. What happened to you continues to encourage the prisoners serving their sentences here."

"Warden, I appreciate the care I received during my seven years here," Pastor Arakaki, smiling, responded with a bow.

The warden brought out his file on Saburo Arakaki with its bulky documents and correspondence. "Your number was J-608, wasn't it?"

"Yes! J-608! That's it."

The warden pulled out two photographs taken on the day Saburo was admitted to Oahu Prison; they showed side and front views of Saburo Arakaki holding a plaque displaying his prisoner ID number, J-608. He looked very young—hair parted to one side, well-groomed, straight posture—but anxiety showed in his eyes.

Miike thumbed through the pages of material:

Arakaki, Saburo
Serial Number: J-608
Case Number: General Court Martial 2135-80/1dr
Crime: Violation of Section D-14, Naval Courts and Boards, 1937
Sentenced: April 2, 1946
Date of Admission: July 31, 1947
Maximum Sentence: Natural Life
Sex: Male   Age: 20   Height: 5′6″
Nationality: Japanese
Birthplace: Okinawa, April 24, 1927
Eyes: Brown   Hair: Black   Weight: 135.5 lbs
Complexion: Light Brown
Distinguishing features: Scar on jaw, two moles above upper lip, on left side

There were also detailed descriptions of Saburo's personal history—his childhood, educational history, circumstances surrounding his criminal offense, and his deposition. His name is mistakenly recorded as Shingaki on certain papers. Likewise, for some reason, his year of birth is incorrectly recorded as 1927. The correct year is 1926.

The group received special permission to enter the cellblock area with two conditions: that they would not photograph prisoners and that they would follow the instructions of the guard assigned to accompany them.

As the guard guided Pastor Arakaki and Miike toward the cellblock, the camera crew trailed behind. The old group cells and solitary confinement cells were located on the east side of the prison complex. The original main entrance stood to the north of a two-story building with wings that intersected in an X; a long corridor connected this structure with a three-story building. In the center of both buildings, a paved concrete walkway cut across the inner yard at an angle. In the corner of the inner yard stood a white cross twice as high as a man.

"There it is," Pastor Arakaki whispered, looking around. "From here it all looks the same." An armed guard looked down on the group from a tower located above the massive concrete wall; his gaze was piercing.

"Where do we start?" Miike asked.

Pastor Arakaki pointed toward the long three-story building. "My cell was the second solitary cell from the left on the third floor. A guard used to take us up the stairs."

Entry and exit from the cellblock was carefully controlled. The guard contacted the guard station on his walkie-talkie, and the cellblock door was remotely unlocked and locked from the guard station.

Pastor Arakaki and Miike climbed up to the third floor. Walking down the hallway, they entered through an iron-barred door. Convicts peered out from their cells with curiosity. Some called out to the visitors.

The solitary confinement cell in which prisoner J-608 had been held was no longer a cell but a locker room.

"This is the room," Pastor Arakaki murmured. "There, that is the window. And these gray walls; they're just as I remembered them." The iron-barred window was higher than chest-level and very narrow. Very little light came through the window so that the room seemed in shadow.

Pastor Arakaki stood looking out the window. Finally he said softly, "To stand here . . . after forty years. . . ." His voice trailed off, and he stood silently for a moment.

Meanwhile, Miike remained quietly in the background.

"Life imprisonment," Pastor Arakaki continued. "Mr. Miike, can you comprehend the state of mind of a person who faces that?" He was still looking out the window, with his back to Miike. Miike could not come up with a response.

"You can't imagine ever being free again," he said. "You have absolutely no hope of ever getting out of prison."

Miike was silent.

"It's different from being sentenced to death. They're both mental torture. With life imprisonment, you escape the fear of execution, but you find yourself tormented just the same. Desperate. You are locked in here until you die. There is no light at the end of the tunnel."

Miike tried to imagine the hopelessness of the twenty-one-year-old Saburo.

Pastor Arakaki looked closely at the iron bars. "In order to live, you have to have some hope. I had given up." His hand clenched the bars across the window. "I don't know how many times I looked at these bars and seriously thought about hanging myself. Wondered how I could manage to hang myself.

"I even thought of escaping, raping a woman, doing heinous crimes, so that I could die by being shot to death." The pastor's shoulders slumped as if he were twenty-one again and could feel what it was like to want to die that badly.

"I wondered why I should have to do hard labor. When I was reprimanded, I retaliated violently. Hatred and hostility toward Americans seethed within me. Gradually, I was becoming psychologically unstable—driven mad. 'I hate this! I hate this! Get me out of here!' I would scream."

Chapter 16

Something to Read

As Saburo frantically tried to escape, shells exploded one after another, each landing closer and closer as if they knew where he was and were chasing him. He was desperate to get away. "Run!" he screamed to himself. "Run for your life or the shells will get you!" Suddenly, he stood on the brink of a cliff. One step, and he would go tumbling into the void. "Help!" He heard the scream fading as he fell to his death. . . .

The violent pounding of his heart awakened him. He lay on his cot, dripping with sweat, in his cell in Oahu Prison. It was midnight. The scenes of that day when he was forced to the edge of Marpi Cliff had been so vivid in his nightmare. He had seen the women throwing themselves off the cliff. He had seen again—in vivid reality—the girl wearing the blue shirt as she vanished from this world in the flash and thunder of exploding shells. "Kill me, oh, please kill me!" The insane screams of the women still rang in his ears—the screams of children as if they were being torn to pieces.

Even awake, the memories couldn't be turned off.

He remembered thinking, *Hell. This is what it is, a living hell,* as he had gazed far out across the open sea. He recalled the faint light that had appeared in the vagueness of the haze. Seven colors forming themselves into a rainbow above the sea and gradually approaching nearer and nearer. A rainbow over hell.

He could see himself looking into the sky, feeling the gentle shower of rain. How good it felt, how for a fleeting moment his anxiety fled and he was free from terror!

Why was I spared? His tortured thoughts tumbled around in his mind. *I have seen many hells. Tapotchau was a mountain of death, and a valley of death. A piece of shrapnel passed through my jaw missing my brain by only a few centimeters. Why? Why did I so narrowly escape death only to be sentenced to death and then saved from execution? Was my life miraculously sustained for some destined purpose? Why am I alive today?*

The threat of execution no longer hangs over me, but there is no way out of this hell of life imprisonment. There is no hope. No future. It's like being strangled gradually, bit by bit. I'd rather die quickly.

I can't sleep, and when I do I have nightmares. There is nowhere to look except at these gray walls and through those iron bars in the window. When morning comes, it will be just the start of another long day of misery locked up here in this dungeon. No matter how hard I struggle, there is no way out of this hell.

Such thoughts put Saburo into insanelike rages. During these times he was more than the guards could handle.

One day, Saburo was called into the prison warden's office. He was sure he was going to receive some kind of disciplinary action. The warden's office was located on the first floor, next to the north entrance.

Warden Joe C. Harper was a friendly person who had the appearance of a teacher. He looked at Saburo with a serious expression. He motioned to a chair. "Have a seat."

It was an unexpected, gentle voice. Saburo bowed in greeting and sat down.

Warden Harper, speaking through a Nisei Japanese-American interpreter, said, "Saburo Arakaki. I am concerned on your behalf. You committed a crime due to the war. You're a very unusual case among the convicts here at Oahu Prison."

Saburo's jaw stiffened. *It is because of you Americans that I am forced to be in this wretched place,* he thought. The hatred in his heart had only intensified over time.

"I became concerned when I received the report describing the circumstances of your sentencing. You may think that you will never be able to get out of here, but there is some hope."

He's just saying that; I won't be deceived.

"You need to genuinely work hard to obey the regulations and do your job well. Understood?"

"Yes," Saburo answered, but his voice lacked conviction.

Shortly thereafter, he was transferred from solitary confinement to the group block. This cellblock was divided into many rooms; approximately eighty convicts of many races—whites, blacks, Polynesians, Japanese, Chinese, and Filipinos—lived together in one area. Tattoos of snakes and hawks were conspicuous on the arms of many of the convicts. In the atmosphere of the tumultuous cellblock, Saburo actually became increasingly unstable psychologically, unable to find the tranquility that he so needed. He didn't understand English and could not make himself understood to others. Whenever anybody touched him or picked a quarrel with him, Saburo reacted violently, like a mad dog with bared fangs. He had a reputation of being dangerous, a murderer whose mind was a little touched. Everyone avoided him. Even in the cellblock Saburo was isolated, and he grew more and more hostile to others.

His bed was his only personal territory. Threatened by loneliness and despair, Saburo retreated to a corner of the cell, shutting out all others. He breathed only because he existed.

What saved him was vegetable gardening—a job at the prison farm. After all, he was from a farming family in Okinawa, and he had studied agriculture at the Saipan Vocational School. Although it had been only a brief interlude, he had worked in the vegetable garden at the Susupe camp as well and found it refreshing and relaxing. On Oahu, the farm was located south of the prison. There, working the soil, sweat pouring from his forehead, Saburo was able to forget his loneliness. Planting seeds and nurturing the seedlings when they sprouted was pure enjoyment. Vegetable gardening was his expertise. The guard who supervised the farm began to take note of him.

It was always summer in Hawaii, yet even on a sunny day gentle showers washed the land. Saburo took pleasure in letting the natural showers soak into his parched body. When he looked up, there would often be a rainbow in the sky, and he would think back to the cliff on Saipan—the rainbow at Marpi. Like there, a rainbow hung over another hell here in Hawaii.

Saburo spoke to no one. Day after day, he sealed off his heart. During break time, the hall was open to the inmates, and movies or concerts would be presented on the stage. Convicts from all the cellblocks gathered there to spend their free time. But even there, Saburo was alone.

One day, about a year after Saburo arrived at Oahu Prison, a thin, small-framed man approached Saburo. He looked Japanese, and although he was young, his eyes seemed strangely old. "Good afternoon, Mr. Arakaki. I'm Kamikawa," he said.

"Hello." Saburo replied. It was all he could bring himself to say.

Kamikawa smiled, "You are always by yourself. That's too bad."

The way you speak Japanese is so stupid. Dumb second-generation Japanese-American, thought Saburo. *What do you want anyway?* The look he gave the man caused Kamikawa to wilt for an instant. As always, his hatred for Americans smoldered deep in Saburo's heart. *I killed two Americanized traitors,* he reminded himself.

Saburo had always felt strangely repulsed by second-generation Japanese-Americans. And the way they spoke Japanese made him feel uneasy. Kamikawa sensed his feelings and grinned wryly. "My Japanese is no good, huh? But I think we can still become friends."

Saburo ignored him. *What is this guy scheming anyway? Why is he trying to get close to me?* Saburo had become very suspicious.

"Saburo, you really should learn English. I can teach you."

Saburo did not answer, and Kamikawa eventually left. More than a week later, however, he again approached Saburo during their break.

"Hi, Saburo. How are you?" he called out cheerfully.

"Oh, hello," answered Saburo. He couldn't help wondering what kind of crime this man could have committed; he had such a gentle smile.

"Saburo, you should read this." Kamikawa handed him a thin pamphlet. Saburo took a quick glance at it; it was written in English.

"What's this, Kamikawa-san?"

"Just call me Danny. This is part of a correspondence course on Christianity."

"On what?"

"Christianity."

"Jesus? That's a Westerner's religion! I hate it!" Saburo spat out.

"Well, it's been really, really good for me."

"I don't want this junk! Besides it is in English. I can't read it." Saburo thrust the paper back at him.

About a week and a half later, Danny Kamikawa came back with another pamphlet. He handed it to Saburo with a smile.

"Saburo, this one's in Japanese."

"Japanese!" Saburo reached for it. His eyes hadn't fallen on Japanese reading materials for more than three years. He had been starving for something—anything—to read in Japanese. It didn't really matter whether it was a newspaper, magazine, or anything, as long as it was in Japanese. Flipping through the pamphlet, he noticed the words *Voice of Prophecy Bible Correspondence Course* on the cover.

"What is this anyway?"

"It's something about the Bible. It would be good for you to read."

"I told you I hate Christianity!"

Danny nodded with a troubled look on his face. But Saburo did crave the chance to read something written in Japanese.

"Kamikawa-san, would it be OK for me to read it even if I don't believe in Christianity?"

"Oh, sure! You don't have to believe it. Just go ahead and read it. Just read it." Danny smiled.

Saburo took the pamphlet to his bunk, thinking he would just read it and then throw it away. It was only a few pages, anyway. He had missed seeing Japanese characters. As he read his native language, each word seemed to be instantly absorbed into his parched heart and mind: "The Bible is one of the classics in literature. The most ancient portions of the Bible date back to about 3,500 years B.C., and the newest portion was written about 1,900 years ago. It is truly an ancient book, but it has continued to be read even today. In it is something precious that captivates the hearts of people. In it is hidden the profound wisdom of God. Given a choice of one book to read, many would choose the Bible. No matter how many times one reads the Bible, there is always fresh meaning in its words—words that will satisfy the longings of the heart."

These words sank into Saburo's heart like precious droplets of water soaking into the arid desert sands. He read on, brushing aside the thought that this was the Christian's Bible he was reading about.

Chapter 17

An Unexpected Visitor

"Kamikawa-san, I read that paper through—many times over, in fact. I think I want to read more."

"That's great, Saburo." Danny responded, a smile spreading across his face. Every few days he brought more material, and Saburo continued reading like he was obsessed.

He skipped over the parts he didn't understand or couldn't accept and plunged on. Unconsciously, his hatred toward this "Western religion" began to melt away. He read about a man called Jesus who was nailed to a cross and killed. A man who was totally innocent, not guilty of any crime, yet who was sentenced to death and executed. Saburo learned that this Man died to save sinful humanity, that He died in our place. He read that whoever accepts this and believes in Jesus Christ will be forgiven of his sins and be saved.

Within a few weeks, Saburo had finished the first section of the correspondence course. He reread it several times.

Who is this Jesus anyway? It says that He is the Son of God. It was difficult for him to believe. But he wanted to read the Bible to find out more.

"Kamikawa-san. I really wish I had a Bible."

Danny's narrow eyes grew wide, and his face lit up with joy.

"Oh, Saburo! That's great! But English is no good, right? You want a Japanese Bible. OK. I'll see what I can do. But it won't be easy to get a Japanese Bible; you'll have to be patient."

That night as he slept, he dreamed that two military policemen suddenly grabbed him by the arms and pulled him out of his cell. He saw a single, wooden pillar erected in front of a gray concrete wall. The policemen tied his arms behind him, and before he knew it, he was bound to the pillar.

"Hey! Wait! Wait a minute! What are you trying to do to me?" he tried to shout, but no sound came from his throat. He was blindfolded, and then everything went black.

"Please, this can't be real! My sentence was reduced! I'm not supposed to be shot to death!"

He heard the sound of the rifle bolt being engaged.

"Wait! Wait!"

There was no answer. He heard someone bark out the order to fire! Saburo screamed, kicking the ground—and waking himself up.

His heart was racing. A small night lamp illuminated the dark ceiling of the cellblock. He heard the snoring of men around him. He slowly calmed his heavy breathing. Unable to fall back sleep, he began to think. *Jesus didn't kill anyone, but He was executed. I killed two people. Even now I can hear their last cries. It was for the emperor, for my country. I obeyed an order to kill. That shouldn't be a sin.*

So he had told himself up to now. But what about that deep uneasiness that still bothered him, deep within his heart?

The one who ordered me to kill betrayed me and ran off scot-free. Was his command right? Did I really kill for the emperor and my country? Japan was defeated in the war. That's a fact. And if so . . . what does this mean? Did I really commit a crime?

Now wide awake, Saburo mulled these things over in his mind. He got up and walked over to the window. Outside, a faint light was beginning to pierce the clouds in the early morning eastern sky.

"J-608!" the guard called out at the doorway to the cell. "Get out! The storage chief wants to see you." Saburo had no idea what was going on, but he followed the guard.

The storage chief looked Japanese-American or Chinese. He brought out a green military bag from the depths of the storage room. "J-608. Is this yours?"

Saburo saw the nametag on the bag: "Saburo Arakaki." He nodded.

"Look inside. If you don't need anything, we'll toss it. OK?"

Saburo opened the bag and looked inside. The old shorts that he had used in the Guam prison. Underwear. A tattered towel. Things that he had no use for. He was about to say that he did not need any of it, but then he decided to reach deep down inside the bag—just in case there was something else there. As he thrust his hand into the bag, his fingers caught on something rectangular.

He took the object out. He could not believe his eyes. It was his "pillow" from the Guam prison. Sure enough, on the cover, in Japanese kanji characters were the words "The New Testament of the Bible."

"Aha!" he shouted.

The storage chief and the guard were baffled.

"I found it! I found it! It's here!" Saburo held the Bible up high in the air and leaped about in excitement. "I can't believe it! I found a Bible. I found it!"

He couldn't help but feel moved. The storage chief looked bewildered. He gestured with his finger at his head. "Is he crazy or something?" The guard shrugged.

Something that Saburo never thought could happen had happened. The Bible that he wanted so much was there before his eyes. He could not believe it. Even after returning to his cell, he could not contain his excitement.

"What happened? What's up with him?" his fellow prisoners wondered.

Saburo opened his Bible. It was written in a literary style that wasn't always easy to read. *Where to start?* He had no clue. Nonetheless he began reading.

Several days later the guard called again, "J-608! You have a visitor."

"A visitor? For me?" *Who could it be?* Saburo didn't know anyone in Hawaii outside the prison. With curiosity written all over his face, he headed to the visitation room.

A distinguished gentleman waited him. He was a Japanese man who appeared to be in his sixties, his hair streaked with gray, impeccably dressed in a suit and a conservative tie. The moment Saburo stepped into the room, the man broke into a warm smile.

"How do you do? Are you Mr. Arakaki?"

"Yes," Saburo replied, bowing.

The dignified gentleman motioned to Saburo to take a seat. "I am Miyake—Pastor Miyake. I heard from the Bible Correspondence Course office that there was a person in Oahu Prison who was earnestly studying the Japanese Bible Correspondence Course. Actually, I was the one who translated the material into Japanese."

"Really? You translated it?" Saburo was astonished.

"Yes. If I can be of any help to you in your study of the Bible. . . ." he paused. "That's really why I wanted to meet you."

Pastor Miyake spoke beautiful Japanese, something Saburo had not heard for so long. That alone thrilled him. "I am very grateful for your visit," he said.

"Did you know that there is a Bible study group here in the prison? It's in English, of course."

"Is Danny Kamikawa in it?"

"That's right. Danny repented of his sins and became a Christian. He is a model prisoner here."

Saburo nodded. Pastor Miyake continued, "If you wish, I will ask the warden to arrange for you to have some time for Bible studies in Japanese."

"Can you? Please do." It was all so unexpected.

"Mr. Arakaki. If you don't mind, would you tell me about the experiences you've gone through up to this point?" Pastor Miyake peered over his round glasses at Saburo with a kindly expression.

Falteringly at first, Saburo began to speak about being born in Okinawa, how he had fought against the American forces as a student in the Saipan Vocational School, how he killed a person in the civilian concentration camp and then killed another in the mountains. He told how he was arrested after the Japanese surrender to the United States and that in court he had been convicted and sentenced to be executed. Then in Guam his sentence had been reduced to life imprisonment. And finally, for reasons he did not understand, he was sent to Hawaii.

Pastor Miyake's gaze fell. He had been listening carefully, nodding with understanding. Finally he raised his face and spoke. "Mr. Arakaki . . ." His eyes filled with tears. Saburo was bewildered. "Can I ask you a question? How old were you when you committed murder?"

"I was nineteen."

"Why did you kill?" The voice that asked was gentle, but the question was difficult and severe.

"I was commanded to do so by a military policeman."

"Ordered to do so? For what reason?"

"For the emperor." Saburo tried to say "for the emperor and my country," but the words choked in his throat. Until very recently, he had fully believed that the murder that he had committed was proper. But as he studied the Bible, he began to see that it was a tragic mistake. He knew what he had done was not right.

"I . . . I . . ." Saburo tried to answer, but could not. Pastor Miyake waited silently.

"I . . ." Saburo looked into the eyes of Pastor Miyake. "I made a terrible mistake. A sin. I committed a sin." Saburo's voice trembled, and tears flowed from his eyes. Tears rolled down the cheeks of Pastor Miyake, too, as he nodded in agreement.

Here is someone who actually cries with me. A powerful, fiery emotion spread through Saburo's heart. For a long while, the thoughts in the room refused expression in words.

Then, quietly, almost in a whisper, Pastor Miyake said, " 'For some reason I was shipped to Hawaii. . . .' Isn't that what you said? 'For some reason . . .'?"

"Yes."

"You were sent to Hawaii to serve your prison term. You didn't want to come. Given the choice, you would prefer to have been sent to Japan?"

"That's right."

The pastor closed his eyes. He remained quietly meditative for a long moment. "Arakaki-san . . ."

"Yes?"

"Perhaps you did not come to Hawaii just to serve your prison term."

Saburo didn't understand.

"I believe you came so that you would encounter the Bible."

"What?" Saburo felt something like an electric shock travel through his body.

"I believe you came here in order to meet God. Just now, that is what I have come to think," Pastor Miyake said, looking intently at Saburo.

The statement brought Saburo to his feet. It was as if a flash of light had penetrated his consciousness.

Chapter 18

New Life

Major changes were beginning to take place in Saburo's life. His study of the Bible quickly intensified. He also began studying English with Danny Kamikawa. On Saturday afternoons, Pastor Shohei Miyake visited without fail—always dressed in a suit, even in hot weather. He studied the Bible with Saburo and answered his questions.

Pastor Miyake had been sent to Hawaii from Japan before the war as a missionary to believers in Hawaii. He had recently retired from active service as a church pastor. Soon church members, Kazunobu Okuda, James Suyeoka, and even the elder of the church, began to visit Saburo to bring him encouragement. Pastors Hideo Oshita and Nobuo Nomi also supported Saburo in his search for answers from the Bible.

Something was troubling Saburo. "Pastor Miyake," he said, "in the general cellblock it is always noisy, and that bothers me. I wish there were a quiet spot for prayer."

Pastor Miyake nodded understandingly, but he knew that wish would be difficult to grant in a prison. "Let's pray to God about it. Read what it says here in the Gospel of Matthew." He opened his Bible and pointed out a verse. "Ask, and it will be given to you; seek, and you will find; knock, and it will be opened to you" (Matthew 7:7).

After Saburo had read the verse out loud, the pastor explained. "These are the words of Jesus. God has promised this."

"Promised?"

"The New Testament is the part of the Bible that was written after the birth of Jesus Christ. The word *testament* means 'covenant' or 'promise'—God's promise to us human beings."

God's promise . . . Seek and ye shall find. . . . While Saburo turned this thought over in his mind, something else flashed into his thinking. After returning to the cellblock, he tried to express his request to the guard in English, using hand and arm motions. "This is Bible," he said, holding up the book. "I read. I pray. Jesus Christ. Do you understand? Jesus Christ. I want, please, place! Quiet place." The guard, shaking his head, walked away.

"I guess it's useless," Saburo sighed. Just then the guard returned with a Japanese-American staff member who could speak Japanese. Perhaps the guard was moved by the earnestness of Saburo's appeal.

"Please, I would like to have a quiet place where I can read my Bible and pray. Could you please request this of Warden Harper?" Saburo appealed fervently. And he continued to pray to God. "Please, Lord, please provide me with a place of prayer."

About a week later, Saburo, accompanied by the same guard and staff member, was led down into a basement room located below the intersection of the two cellblock wings. It was fenced off and being used as a storage area. The staff opened the wire screen door to the room. "J-608, Saburo Arakaki, is granted permission by the warden to enter this room for prayer. All guards will be notified of this," the staff member told him.

"Oh, thank you very much! Thank you! I am so thankful! Thank you!" Saburo was moved with emotion and shook hands vigorously with the guard and the staff member. The guard grinned at his unrestrained joy, while the Japanese-American staff member patted Saburo on the shoulder with a smile.

God must have heard my prayer! Saburo was filled with wonder.

Under a single light bulb in that dark basement room, shielded from the noise and crudeness of the cellblock, Saburo spent more and more time studying his Bible. The Bible verses that he read penetrated deep into his heart.

" 'For God so loved the world that He gave His only begotten Son, that whoever believes in Him should not perish but have everlasting life' " (John 3:16).

The Bible says that God is love and that He will forgive sinners. I killed two people. Realizing the enormity of the sin that he had committed, Saburo was strangely drawn to the words of the Bible. He didn't believe that he could be forgiven just by reading the words of the Bible, yet somehow those words seemed to bring healing and a peace to him.

One day, Saburo reached the twelfth chapter of the Gospel of John. He read, " 'I have come as a light into the world, that whoever believes in Me should not abide in darkness. And if anyone hears My words and does not believe, I do not judge him; for I did not come to judge the world but to save the world' " (John 12:46, 47).

Jesus says that if people hear His words but do not keep His words, He does not judge them. That He came not to judge, but to save the world. A sinner can be saved. He read the verses over and over again.

"I have come as a light into this world . . ." And as Saburo read those words, a deep emotion overflowed from his heart, and he was moved to tears. He dropped to the ground and knelt in prayer. Looking up, he cried out, "God, thank You so much!"

A year and a half had passed since his imprisonment at Oahu Prison. Warden Harper and the guards were amazed to witness the transformation of prisoner J-608. Saburo was awarded a pin for being an exemplary prisoner, and he was allowed more freedom in his movements within the prison.

One day, Saburo stood before Warden Harper. "Warden, I have a request to make."

"I knew that you would come to see me sometime, Saburo," the warden replied with a smile.

"Warden, I would like to be excused from working on Saturday."

"Why should I excuse you from Saturday work?"

"Seventh-day Adventists keep the Ten Commandments in the Bible. The fourth commandment says that the seventh day of the week, Saturday, is the Sabbath."

"I know."

"I would like to keep the Sabbath and rest from work, and so please let me have the day as a day for prayer. Please grant me my request."

Warden Harper studied Saburo's eyes intently.

"I have already been thinking about this, Saburo. Granting your request would certainly be a special allowance. But if you are going to be a true Seventh-day Adventist Christian, it is necessary for you to keep the Sabbath. I'm very pleased with your record here. So I will permit you to take Saturdays off from your work."

"Thank you very much, Warden! I appreciate it very much."

Of the thousand or more prisoners in this facility, only Saburo was granted such a special privilege. His was definitely a rare case.

Sometime afterwards, Saburo was reading his Bible when he came across these words: " 'Our Father in heaven, hallowed be Your name. Your kingdom come. Your will be done on earth as it is in heaven. Give us this day our daily bread. And forgive us our debts, as we forgive our debtors. And do not lead us into temptation, but deliver us from the evil one. For yours is the kingdom and the power and the glory forever. Amen' " (Matthew 6:9–13).

According to these verses, the Bible is saying that if I forgive someone their sins against me, then God will also forgive me. But if I don't forgive, God in heaven will not forgive me either. A face surfaced in Saburo's mind—the face of MP Corporal Jojima on Saipan, the man who had commanded him to commit murder and who had then betrayed him, escaped, and placed the blame for the crime on him. The burning desire in Saburo's heart to tear him to pieces, limb from limb, had not disappeared from his heart. *If that man appeared before me right now, I don't know what I'd do. But I probably will never, ever meet him again.*

He had not thought much about the sinful nature that human beings are born with. But the knowledge that he had committed murder twice weighed heavily on his heart. *The agony that I suffered fighting against approaching death as a convict on death row can't possibly compare with the final agony of those two that I killed,* he thought. *Now the only thing I can do is to ask for forgiveness from God and pray that they rest in peace.*

"Therefore, if anyone is in Christ, he is a new creation; old things have passed away; behold, all things have become new" (2 Corinthians 5:17). The hope to be born again through Christ burgeoned in Saburo's heart.

One day, as Saburo and Pastor Miyake walked through the prison yard together, Saburo turned and said, "Pastor, I want to be baptized."

Pastor Miyake stopped and looked closely at Saburo.

Saburo wasn't kidding.

"But, what should I do? There is no water tank in the prison large enough to submerge my whole body. The bathrooms have only showers, no tubs. I checked the kitchen, too. There is only a drum can."

Saburo had learned from the Bible that baptism symbolizes the death and resurrection of Jesus Christ. When one is buried beneath the water, he is saying that he is dying to sin, and as he rises out of the water, he is saying that he wants to come up as a new person to live a new life. Saburo knew that true baptism meant submerging the whole body, not just sprinkling water on the head. What could be done? There didn't seem to be any obvious solution.

"Pastor, shall I dig a hole that can hold the water?" Saburo pointed to the prison yard. He was dead serious.

"Why don't we pray to God?" Pastor Miyake suggested.

"That's right! Ask, and it shall be given." Saburo's eyes brightened as he spoke.

"Just as you asked for Sabbaths off work, why don't you approach the warden and ask him about baptism. I will also pray," the pastor said.

Saburo made the request, but could a water tank really be installed somewhere in the prison, and could a baptism ceremony really take place? This troubled him. About this same time, in March 1949, he was named the group leader for the prison farm. He made job assignments and work plans. This responsibility also weighed on his shoulders. A year and eight months had passed since his arrival in Hawaii.

One day Saburo was called into Warden Harper's office once again. "Saburo, I'm giving you permission to go to the Japanese Seventh-day Adventist Church in Honolulu to be baptized," the warden announced.

For a moment, Saburo could not believe it. Then he quickly thanked the warden.

Looking sternly at Saburo, and enunciating each word slowly and clearly, the warden said, "Saburo, I want to believe that you will not make a mistake."

Saburo wasn't sure what he meant by those words, but he was very appreciative of the warden's decision.

On April 2, the day of the baptism, Saburo appeared in the warden's office early in the morning. Warden Harper looked at Saburo in his prison outfit and shook his head. "Can't we come up with a suit that fits you?" he wanted to know. Someone remembered a suit belonging to a Filipino that should be the right size. It was quickly brought from the storage room to the warden's office.

For the first time in his life, Saburo put on a suit and tie, both of which were borrowed.

Again, the warden looked sternly at Saburo. "Saburo, you will be going to the church alone today."

"What!" Saburo couldn't believe his ears.

"I will send you over in my own car," the warden stated, breaking out into a smile for the first time.

The warden's Cadillac rolled toward the church on Keaumoku Street. The driver was the only guard assigned to Saburo. He was completely unarmed, without even a sidearm, much less handcuffs. And like Saburo, he was dressed in a suit. The guard pulled up at the curb and pointed toward the church building in front. "That's the Japanese church, Saburo. Go ahead. I'll stay here."

Saburo was again surprised. "Alone? By myself?" All at once he realized how much the warden was trusting him, how much he thought of him, and counted on him. A warm feeling filled Saburo's heart. Somehow, the ill feelings that he harbored against Americans seemed to be slipping away.

A convicted murderer, formerly on death row and now serving a life sentence, was traveling beyond the prison walls to church to be baptized—totally unguarded. This was unheard of. Unimaginable.

As if in a dream, Saburo stepped into the worship sanctuary. The many Japanese-American church members welcomed him with warm applause. Following the worship service, he slipped into a black baptismal gown.

Pastor Shohei Miyake conducted the baptismal service. "My dear Brother Saburo, do you believe that the Lord Jesus Christ is your personal Savior?" he asked.

"I do," Saburo responded with conviction.

The baptismal font behind the pulpit was filled with water. Saburo entered the font accompanied by Pastor Miyake. The cool water came up to his chest, but in his heart he again felt a warmth springing up inside. Pastor Miyake took Saburo's hands in his left hand, and raised his right arm above Saburo's head. "My dear Brother Saburo. Because of your expression of faith in Jesus Christ, I, as a minister of the gospel, now baptize you in the name of the Father, the Son, and the Holy Spirit. Amen."

"Amen." Saburo closed his eyes. Pastor Miyake supported Saburo's neck with his hand. Saburo held his breath, his hands resting on the pastor's arm. And then Saburo's body was buried in the water. His old life of sin had died.

Then, supported by the pastor's arm, Saburo rose out of the water. He stepped out of the baptismal font—born again, granted new life, his heart washed clean.

As a chorus of hymns flowed through the church, Saburo stood quietly. The baptismal water dripping from his face mingled with tears of joy that welled up from his heart.

Chapter 19

Could Pardon Be Possible?

"After I was baptized, even the air in this walled-in prison world seemed different." Pastor Arakaki and Miike stood in the courtyard of the Oahu Prison. Staring up at the ceiling of the solitary confinement cell on the third floor where he was first imprisoned, Pastor Arakaki explained, "I can still distinctly remember those days of raging despair, but at the same time, it seems like it was just a nightmare, a bad dream, from which I awoke."

Miike nodded.

It must have been recess time, because convicts began to spill out into the courtyard in groups of two or three. They stopped and looked curiously toward the Japanese visitors. Pastor Arakaki approached them, smiling warmly. "Hello, friends!"

The convicts seemed a bit surprised, but responded to Pastor Arakaki's warm smile. "Hi."

"I was in here forty years ago," Pastor Arakaki said in English.

"As a guard?"

"No, as a lifer."

"What for? What did you do?"

"Murder. Two persons."

The convicts shouted with surprise and gathered around Pastor Arakaki. "I first received a death sentence because of a war crime."

"A death sentence?" the convicts again raised their voices. "What are you doing now, and where are you now?"

"I am a pastor now, in Japan."

"A pastor! That's incredible! Really?" the convicts gestured excitedly, their voices gaining volume.

Pastor Arakaki nodded with a smile. "I came into contact with the Bible in here for the first time. My sins were forgiven by Jesus Christ. It would be good for you, too, if you read the Bible."

One of the convicts wanted to shake hands with Pastor Arakaki. When the pastor responded with a smile, the other convicts also came, one after another, to shake his hand.

Miike watched and let his mind wander back thirty-eight years.

* * * * *

Danny Kamikawa had completed his sentence and was being released from prison. On that special day, Saburo was out working on the farm; he did not have the chance to say his final goodbyes to Danny. Saburo had encountered the Bible through Danny, who had also been foremost in sharing Saburo's joy after baptism.

With Danny gone, Saburo decided to try to share with his fellow inmates the peace and happiness he felt in his heart after his baptism—just like Danny had done. He began to encourage his fellow convicts to take the Bible correspondence course. He requested Pastor Miyake to send him a quantity of correspondence course booklets and went through the cell-blocks, using his broken English and hand gestures, earnestly encouraging his fellow convicts to study the lessons. "I'm very happy, because of Bible. I study this. I believe Jesus Christ. You understand? You study this. You study this."

Although many ignored him with wry smiles, there were some who had witnessed his amazing transformation and who remembered how he had earlier been like a rabid dog. These prisoners accepted the Bible correspondence course. As a result, around two hundred convicts began attending a Bible study group.

Pastor Oshita brought word to Saburo that an effort was underway to have his sentence reduced. At this unexpected news, Saburo's heart overflowed with gratitude. But at this time there was sad news as well. After his transfer to Hawaii, Saburo had been writing letters to Okinawa, trying to find out what had happened to his family during the war.

In April 1945, much of Okinawa had been reduced to ashes after a fierce three-month ground battle with the landing American forces. Much as had happened in Saipan, many people in Okinawa resorted to sacrificing their own lives rather than surrendering to the enemy. More than one hundred thousand civilians died in these fierce battles that swept over them.

Finally, the long-awaited response to Saburo's letters arrived. His mother and grandmother had both been caught up in the whirlwinds of the war and had died. His sisters and brother, however, were still alive and were being cared for by distant relatives. Saburo's father, who had tried to find a way out of deep poverty in Tinian, had also died in a ground battle.

War must be humanity's greatest evil and sin, Saburo told himself. *Look at the countless lives it has destroyed.* He couldn't help wishing for a peace-filled world in which war would never rise up again. And he realized that the only thing that could sustain peace in the world was the love of God that he had come to know in his heart.

In 1950, Saburo heard from Pastor Miyake that evangelism had begun in Okinawa. "Sensei," he said, "I will work in Okinawa to help spread the gospel message!" It was a thought that seemed to spring from his heart and lips before he knew what he would say. Looking at him, Pastor Miyake nodded, but the hope expressed by this convict—sentenced to life imprisonment—amazed him.

"Sensei, I'll pray to God! 'Seek, and you shall find . . .' the Bible says!"

"That's right," Pastor Miyake replied. "Let's pray."

Pastor Miyake took Saburo's hands, and they bowed their heads in the dark basement room of the prison. Saburo prayed earnestly. "Dear God, please get me out of here! I will work for the evangelism of Okinawa. I promise to dedicate my life to spreading Your gospel. Please God, get me out of here!"

Saburo continued to pray day after day. But the days passed with no change. *My prayer—could it be just a wish for selfish reasons?* Doubts and perplexities crept into his mind, and he began to feel troubled. *Maybe they will reduce my sentence—but only after I am an old man.* These disquieting thoughts plagued him. Saburo opened his Bible: "Be anxious for nothing, but in everything by prayer and supplication, with thanksgiving, let your requests be made known to God" (Philippians 4:6). "Commit your works to the Lord, and your thoughts will be established" (Proverbs 16:3).

Saburo continued to pray fervently.

* * * * *

Miike looked through the copies of the papers and correspondence in the file of Saburo Arakaki, prisoner J-608. There were 161 pages, about half of which were letters concerning the application for reduced sentence. Attached to these letters was the psychiatrist's evaluation. Warden Harper had repeatedly sent applications for a reduction in Saburo's sentence to Washington, D.C. But each time, the request had been rejected by either the U.S. Naval Correction Board or the Secretary of the Navy.

Finally, in a letter dated March 29, 1951, Warden Harper made a direct appeal to President Harry Truman for a reduction of sentence in a letter that clearly demonstrated his opinion of the inmate under his jurisdiction.

> Honorable Harry S. Truman
> President of the United States
> The White House
> Washington, D.C.
> Re: Saburo Arakaki

Sir:

The above-named individual was convicted of murder in the first degree by a Military Commission for Civil Affairs, Island of Saipan, on April 2, 1946, and was sentenced to hang.

He was later transferred to the Guam stockade, his sentence commuted to life imprisonment, and Oahu Prison designated as his place of confinement. He was received by us on July 31, 1947. His prison record since that time has been exemplary in every respect.

We submit herewith copies of correspondence we have had with the Corrective Services Branch, U.S.N., institutional reports, various other data, and direct your attention particularly to the copies of psychiatric examinations contained in the enclosures.

This man's case was considered by the Navy Sentence Review and Clemency Board in April 1949, and by the Secretary of the Navy during October, 1950. Both resulted in negative action.

Despite this, we continue to feel that we are incarcerating a man who is not inherently a criminal, whose offense was committed when he was only seventeen years of age, during war time, and shortly after he learned that his father was killed during the bombing of Tinian by our forces.

We are sorry to disagree with the Secretary of the Navy, a copy of whose letter appears among the enclosures, but we feel that despite the fact that the formal record of evidence is "devoid of any indication that Shingaki was acting under orders at the time he committed the offense of murder", that there is a strong probability that the formal record does not contain all of the facts. Further, we feel that the mitigating circumstances alluded to in the preceding paragraph have not been given the weight they deserve.

This man has now been incarcerated, counting his time on Saipan and Guam, approximately six years. He is still only twenty-three years of age now. For the past four years, he has borne daily contact with habitual criminals without perceptible damage to his own character or to the high purpose he has set for himself.

We believe him to be worthy of consideration and respectfully request the exercise of Executive Clemency in his behalf.

Yours truly,
Joe C. Harper, Warden

* * * * *

Over five years had passed since the end of the war. An occupation policy had been implemented, putting Japan under the authority of the Supreme Commander for the Allied Powers (SCAP), General Douglas MacArthur. In May 1947, a new constitution instituted democracy and pacifism in Japan. In November of the same year, the International Military Tribunal for the Far East (Tokyo Trial) convicted twenty-five Class A suspected war criminals, and in December, executed seven by hanging, including the former prime minister, Hideki Tojo. June 1950 saw the outbreak of the Korean War. The Japanese economy, impoverished by defeat, took a favorable turn, stimulated by the special procurements of goods and services required by the new conflict. The National Police Reserve (later the Self-Defense Force) was established. The occupation purge, officially known as "Removal and Exclusion of Undesirable Personnel from Public Office," which had removed former military personnel, was abolished. U.S. President Harry Truman, stymied by the invasion of Korea by North Korean forces and the introduction of Chinese troops into the war, stated that the use of nuclear weapons could not be ruled out. The new war suddenly escalated in intensity.

The White House rejected Oahu Prison Warden Harper's application for a reduced sentence for Saburo Arakaki. But this did not deter Warden Harper. He continued to direct his efforts toward Washington, D.C., for Saburo's pardon.

In September 1951, the Treaty of Peace with Japan was signed in San Francisco. When the treaty was formally implemented on April 28, 1952, Japan again became an independent nation, recovering her national sovereignty. The occupation of Japan by the Allied Powers ended, replaced by a security alliance with the United States.

President Dwight D. Eisenhower was inaugurated in Washington, D.C., in January 1953.

Warden Harper and Deputy Warden William P. Motts appealed to Samuel W. King, governor of the Territory of Hawaii, for his assistance. Governor King quickly dispatched an investigator to Oahu Prison to inquire about the circumstances surrounding Saburo Arakaki's imprisonment. Upon receiving the reports generated from the inquiry, the governor added his voice to those pleading for clemency for Saburo Arakaki.

Pastor Hideo Oshita also repeatedly petitioned Mr. Thomas O. Glover, chairman of the Department of Justice Board of Parole. By this time, Saburo had many supporters calling for a reduced sentence.

But however grateful Saburo might be, he could only await a decision and continue to pray from his prison cell. He would soon turn twenty-eight.

Chapter 20

No Such Thing as Coincidence

The sky overhead was an intense blue with clouds drifting by. As Saburo worked on the prison farm, suddenly a cooling shower fell from the clouds above—an unexpected, and welcome, reprieve from the hot, wearying farm work. Straightening up, he saw the great arc of a rainbow stretching across the sky beyond the distant palm trees. It seemed to be a heaven-sent blessing, gently moistening and nourishing his heart.

Later Saburo spoke to Pastor Miyake about the rainbow. "There are a lot of rainbows in Hawaii, aren't there, Sensei?"

"Yes. We often see rainbows. The native Hawaiians at one time believed the rainbow to be the symbol of the god of rich harvest," said Pastor Miyake, smiling.

"And rainbows also appear in the Old Testament of the Bible," Saburo persisted. "Remember how God placed a rainbow in the clouds after the Flood that almost destroyed the earth? And how He promised Noah that it was a sign that such a flood would never come again? Sensei!" Saburo exclaimed. "When I was cornered at the top of Marpi Cliff during the all-out attack on Saipan, it was a hell . . . a living hell. But even there I saw a rainbow lifted up above the sea. A rainbow over hell."

"Even there in hell, there was a rainbow," said Pastor Miyake, repeating Saburo's words, and nodding slowly.

"Sensei, I was surrounded by that rainbow. In any hell, however desperate and discouraging, there is always a rainbow."

Pastor Miyake studied Saburo's face for a moment. Finally, he said, "A rainbow over hell . . . you have taught me a great truth. We may experience many forms of hell in life, but a ray of hope always pierces through."

It was now April 1954. Eight years had passed since the day Saburo had been sentenced to death. Nearly eight and a half years had passed since his arrest. As usual, Saburo was in prayer, alone, in the dark basement of the cellblock. "Prisoner J-608! Prisoner J-608!" The voice sounded like it was coming from the ceiling. Looking up, Saburo saw a guard motioning at the top of the stairs.

"The warden's calling for you. It's very urgent. Hurry!"

Saburo ran up the hallway. The warden's door was open, which was unusual, and he stood behind his desk. Entering the room, Saburo stood at attention, catching his breath, while he waited for the warden to speak.

As Saburo watched, a smile spread across the warden's face. *It must be good news,* Saburo thought.

"Please sit, Saburo." The warden motioned for him to take a seat. He picked up the papers that were on his desk. "Saburo," the warden spoke slowly, one word at a time, "You. Go. Home."

Saburo jumped to his feet. "I. Go. Home? I. Go. Home? I go home!" Saburo leaped in the air.

Warden Harper began reading the paper in his hand, "By a clemency order of the President . . ."

"Thank you very much!"

". . . the Board of Parole has . . ."

"Thank you very much!"

". . . placed a condition of deportation . . ."

Shaking with emotion, Saburo's eyes began to overflow with tears of joy. The warden put the paper down. Immediately, Saburo clasped the warden's hand in both of his. "Thank you, very much! Thank you very much!" he shouted, as if he were in rapture. His own eyes welling with tears, Warden Harper could only nod.

Suddenly Saburo dashed from the office shouting, "I go home! I go home!" Not knowing where to place his feet or what to do with his flailing arms, he ran and leaped about the inner yard of the prison. The other inmates looked on in astonishment.

"Catch him! Catch him!" a guard shouted, and he chased after Saburo, mistakenly thinking the man had lost his mind.

"It's all right. Saburo is getting out of prison." The warden's explanation quickly cleared the misunderstanding.

Saburo went down to the basement to pray. Kneeling on the floor, he clasped both hands fervently in prayer. "Dear God, thank You so very much!" he began. Just then, he was overwhelmed by the joy that burst from the depths of his soul; his entire frame shook with what he knew was God's grace. "God, I'm so thankful. I will work for You from now on. I dedicate my life to sharing the gospel in Okinawa." With sobs of happiness and tears of gratitude, Saburo made a promise—his personal covenant—with God.

* * * * *

That place of prayer, located at the bottom of the stairs, to the right of the stairwell, was still being used for storage—a row of lockers, some cardboard boxes, and canvas bags. Pastor Arakaki and Miike stood in the small basement room. In one corner a fan slowly spun.

"Not much has changed. It was here in this room . . . " Pastor Arakaki knelt on the floor, closed his eyes, and clasped his hands. As Miike watched the figure before him, he suddenly felt the presence of an unseen omnipotence. Saburo's prayers had been answered. A presidential pardon was an unthinkable, totally improbable, extraordinary event.

* * * * *

On May 3, 1954, Prisoner J-608, Saburo Arakaki, was released from prison. The U.S. Department of Immigration made arrangements for Saburo to be returned to Japan by airplane. But Saburo's very first destination upon being released from prison was the Japanese Seventh-day Adventist church, located on Keaumoku Street in Honolulu. There, his fellow believers joined him in joyful celebration. Saburo smiled radiantly as layer after layer of white Plumeria leis were placed on his shoulders.

The air overflowed with a sweet fragrance. A department store owned by a Japanese-American sent a new suit as a gift to celebrate his new start in life.

* * * * *

Today, the Japanese Seventh-day Adventist church in Honolulu has moved to Manoa, in a hilly section of the city. Visiting this mother church of his baptism, Pastor Saburo Arakaki, the Holy Bible in one hand, bowed his head in a silent prayer of thanksgiving. Sunlight filtered through the stained glass window, casting a soft radiance on his figure.

According to Miike's sources, Joe C. Harper, the former warden of Oahu Prison, was now living in Kaneohe, a beach-front town north of the Koolau mountain range. The day after learning this, Pastor Arakaki visited Mr. Harper, accompanied by a church elder.

They found Mr. and Mrs. Harper in a cozy home overlooking the ocean. Mr. Harper's thin, withered body rested in an easy chair.

"How are you, Mr. Harper? I'm Saburo Arakaki."

The elderly man was silent, a trace of doubt or confusion in his eyes.

"I'm Saburo Arakaki." Taking the man's thin white hand in his, Pastor Arakaki repeated, "I'm Saburo. Saburo Arakaki."

Mrs. Harper spoke. "Saburo. I remember you clearly. Joe worked relentlessly to have you released from prison."

"I thought of Warden Harper as my father. Mr. Harper, thank you so much! I appreciate all you did for me very much." Again he took the thin hands and clasped them.

Mrs. Harper, leaned over her husband, whispering, "You know this man, honey." A faint smile crossed the aged man's face.

"Warden Harper, I'm Saburo. Do you remember me?" There was no change in Mr. Harper's expression. No indication that he remembered these events of more than thirty years earlier.

Pastor Arakaki, his eyes welling with tears, softly caressed the thin, aged hands. "I'll never forget you, Mr. Harper. Never! Thank you. Thank you."

The next morning, Pastor Matsunami drove the entourage, now heading home, to the airport. "Matsunami-sensei," Miike said, "thank you very much for everything you have done for us while we were here in Hawaii."

Pastor Matsunami responded, "Oh, by the way, did you hear the news on the radio?"

"What news?"

"Your group really came at absolutely the right time."

"Why? What happened?"

"Yesterday, there was a shakedown at Oahu Prison!"

"A shakedown?" Miike questioned.

"Oahu Prison was closed off to the outside yesterday. All visits, all visitors, absolutely prohibited. There was suspicion that contraband had been brought into the prison, so a thorough investigation, or shakedown, took place."

Miike tried to imagine what would have happened if Pastor Arakaki's visit had been postponed by only one day.

"It happens from time to time," Pastor Matsunami continued. "Two years ago some knives, clubs, and marijuana were found. This time, the only things they have found so far have been some butts of marijuana cigarettes. In 1981, when a shakedown took place, it resulted in a riot."

"Just one day later," Miike mused, "and our schedule would have been ruined."

Pastor Matsunami nodded in agreement. "Just one day later . . ."

As Miike reflected back on the trip, he recalled how in Saipan, the search for actual sites had been very difficult—until while searching they had somehow met someone who was able to direct them to their destination and who even acted as a guide. Now, they had been able to go to the prison only a day before it was closed off to all visitors. Were these mere coincidences?

During the return flight from Honolulu to Narita, Japan, Miike turned to Pastor Arakaki and said, "It's been a difficult journey, I know. But things really did turn out smoothly, due to some amazing coincidences."

Pastor Arakaki smiled. "Mr. Miike, there is no such thing as 'coincidence' in the Bible."

Chapter 21

Face to Face With the Betrayer

On May 10, 1954, Saburo landed at Haneda Airport after boarding a transport plane from Honolulu ferrying U.S. troops headed for Korea. From Haneda, he headed directly for Saniku Gakuin College located in the town of Sodegaura in Kimitsu County of Chiba Prefecture. Above all else, Saburo wanted to study theology when he returned to Japan. The Adventist church in Hawaii, knowing of his desire, submitted a request to the college to accept him.

When Saburo arrived on campus, he had a little more than two hundred dollars in his pocket, which he had saved from daily allowances earned while serving his sentence in prison. Some church members in Hawaii had generously offered to cover whatever funds he lacked for schooling. The campus consisted of an elementary school, a junior high school, a high school, and a two-year college; it was located in lush green woodlands. Twenty-eight-year-old Saburo enrolled in the theology department and began his studies alongside students almost ten years younger than he was.

* * * * *

Arriving at Narita International Airport, Miike's group headed for Sodegaura in a rental car. In the years since Saburo's student days, Saniku Gakuin College had been moved to the town of Otaki in Isumi County of Chiba Prefecture. The school and dormitory buildings on the spacious Sodegaura campus now stood empty. Trees towered overhead, and weeds had taken over the lawns. The sound of cicadas filled the air. Miike and Pastor Arakaki strolled through the campus grounds.

"I still remember my first few days on campus, Pastor Arakaki said. "There were elementary students on the campus at the time. I thought they were so cute, but when I tried to approach them, they shrieked and ran away, shouting that the 'murderer' had come." He smiled wryly as Miike searched his face. "I guess there were a lot of rumors about me," he said.

"What did you do?!"

"What could I do? My classmates were wary of me. Especially the junior high school students. They would give me dirty looks. Everybody seemed to be afraid of me and kept their distance. But campus life was heaven compared to living in prison."

Professor Toshio Yamagata was vice president of the college when Saburo enrolled as a theology student. He later became president and currently serves as professor emeritus at Saniku Gakuin College. Pastor Arakaki and Miike went to visit the professor, who has lived near the campus since his retirement. Professor Yamagata, now an elderly man, warmly invited them into his study.

While visiting Hawaii in 1950, Professor Yamagata had met Saburo while he was still in Oahu Prison. Recalling that visit, the professor said that even then he could see an honest, sincere soul in the rough-hewn young man he met in the prison.

Miike asked, "What was the school's reaction when that letter from Hawaii—from the Japanese Adventist church—arrived, asking you to enroll Saburo Arakaki in classes?"

"We could not promise that he would become a minister. But we decided to let him have the chance to study." The professor spoke with eyes full of radiant kindness.

Pastor Arakaki laughed, "Professor, I told Mr. Miike about the small children crying out, 'The murderer is here! The murderer is here!' "

"That was a really bad situation."

"What did you do about it?" Miike asked.

"We asked Mr. Arakaki to give a testimony to the whole group."

"A testimony?"

"Yes, a testimony about his faith in God and how he had met God through his personal life experiences."

"And how did it go?"

"You could see that the students were moved by his story."

"The way everyone looked at me really changed," agreed Pastor Arakaki.

The professor added, "It was clear that Mr. Arakaki, previously dedicated wholeheartedly to the militarism he had been taught, was now a faithful follower of God, whom he had come to know. He had spent nine years of his precious youth in a dark prison. No doubt he experienced anguish, doubt, and disillusionment during that time. Any human being would."

* * * * *

Even after his conversion, Saburo had kept certain strong feelings to himself, unexpressed to anyone. Ever since he had landed at Haneda Airport, a certain man had been on his mind, someone he felt he had to meet—former MP Corporal Takeo Jojima, the man who had ordered him to murder, who had betrayed him in the end and placed the responsibility of the crime on him alone, and who had then gone home.

Saburo composed a letter expressing his desire to meet Jojima and mailed it to Mr. Takeo Jojima's permanent domicile registration office in "A" prefecture. During the brutal U.S. military mop-up operations on Mount Tapotchau in Saipan, when they had been uncertain about whether or not they would survive, Saburo and Jojima had made a vow. If one of them did not make it alive through the battle, the other had promised to find the deceased's surviving relatives and recount the circumstances of his final hours. And so they had hammered into their memories each other's permanent domicile address.

In the Guam prison for war criminals, Saburo had accepted his approaching death. Yet he continued to mull over Jojima's address, although he knew it was in vain. Forget that man? Never. He would not let him get away; he would search for him until death, place him under a death curse, and kill him. Saburo had burned with bitter hatred and resentment.

In response to his letter, a postcard from Jojima's wife arrived at Saburo's dormitory. It said that because of his job, her husband was renting a place in Yodobashi in Tokyo. She had written his new address on the postcard.

Tokyo! That's not very far! Suppressing his impatient feelings, Saburo waited eagerly for the summer school break. On the very first Sunday of vacation, he headed toward Tokyo on the Sobu Line. He got off at Shinjuku Station and headed west.

Nine years had elapsed since the end of the war. Rows of buildings lined Shinjuku, and people crowded in front of a street-side television screen. Store windows showcased the three "dream appliances"—a washing machine, a refrigerator, and a vacuum cleaner. The "pachinko" parlors were filled with gamblers, and the loud hum of military marches spilled from loudspeakers. Advertisement posters competed for attention in a commotion of garish loud colors. Saburo felt that he had somehow strayed onto a different planet.

He stopped to ask directions two or three times. As he passed through the shopping district into a back street, a three-wheeled truck showered him with sand and dust. Large thunderclouds formed in the skies above, and the humidity was stifling. He came to a row of old houses that must have survived the great Tokyo fires in the war.

Saburo stood in front of an old, two-story building that appeared to be a rooming house. *Would Jojima be there?* Saburo paused in front of the building and attempted to quiet his feelings. Thunder pealed in the distance.

Opening the front door, Saburo called out, and the landlady, a woman in her fifties, appeared at the entrance.

"Is Mr. Jojima here?"

"Yes, he lives upstairs. And you are . . .?"

"Please tell him his friend Arakaki is here."

"All right. Just a moment."

The landlady disappeared up the stairs at the end of the building. From the sound of her footsteps, Jojima's room seemed to be on the second floor at the end of the hallway.

"Mr. Jojima. You have a visitor."

Saburo heard the landlady's voice but not the response. The sound of the creaking stairs announced the landlady's return.

"He will be down soon."

"Thank you for your trouble," Saburo bowed.

He waited for a while. Jojima didn't come down. Saburo looked up the stairs. He could hear no sounds of movement. *Maybe he is changing his clothes,* he told himself.

Not knowing what to do, Saburo closed the front door and went back outside to wait. A peal of thunder pierced the quiet. Looking up he saw that gray clouds had gathered in the sky.

Saburo wondered what kind of expression Jojima would have on his face when he appeared. After all, it had been nine years since they had last seen each other. He imagined Jojima coming down the stairs and greeting him with a smile, saying, "It's great to see that you have been well, Arakaki."

Saburo sat down on the stone steps at the entrance to the rooming house and wiped the sweat on his face. Crossing his arms, he waited quietly. It was like it had been in the prison in Guam, when he waited for his punishment to come, tormented by the fear of death and burning with vengeance against Corporal Jojima. It all seemed like a nightmare that had happened long ago.

More than fifteen minutes passed. Jojima had still not appeared. The heated shafts of sunlight faded away. Dark clouds began to encircle the sky. The landlady peeked out. "Mr. Jojima hasn't come down yet?"

"No."

She climbed the stairs again. Thirty minutes had now passed. Apprehension began to grow in Saburo's heart. Lightning flashed above. Peals of thunder reverberated back and forth. *I wonder if he ran away!* Saburo stood up suddenly and rushed to the back of the building. From the way the building was built, it would not be possible to escape from the second floor. He returned to the front and looked up at the window on the second floor. There was laundry hanging out, and no indication of escape.

Jojima had to be in the room.

A gust of wind sent a cloud of dust and sand flying. Saburo sat on the stone step. *I wonder what Jojima is thinking right now. Maybe he thinks I've come to get revenge.*

Jojima was an outstanding and courageous soldier. He bravely volunteered to fight, without a thought for his life. Saburo admired his dedication and commitment to protect his mother country. Saburo's militaristic education had been thorough. As a result, when commanded to, he committed two crimes—murders—believing that it was for the emperor and for his country.

Jojima, too, had undergone a militaristic education. Both had survived those years of war. And both had to carry the weight of misery that came during those years of war.

When the war ended, human weakness and shrewdness could cause one even to betray others in order to escape death. That, too, was a result of the sinful nature with which human beings are born. *Jojima must have been living with much the same kind of misery I've endured,* Saburo thought. *The only deliverance from that misery is God's love.*

Saburo turned around quickly, instinctively feeling that the door was being opened behind him. There stood Takeo Jojima. Saburo got to his feet and stood face to face with him.

Jojima stood silently, his face looking down toward the ground. Saburo forgot the words that he had felt he should say.

After a long moment, Jojima slowly lifted his face. He looked haggard; his eyes were dark. His pale face betrayed a heart trembling with fear.

"Mr. Jojima," Saburo called out.

The eyes that looked back at him flashed fear.

"It's me, Saburo Arakaki."

Jojima just nodded.

"It's been a long time."

Jojima lowered his eyes, saying nothing.

"I escaped execution. . . . I've returned safely."

Jojima was silent.

"Please, don't be afraid of me."

Jojima raised his face and looked at Saburo with suspicion. Saburo continued speaking, "I am no longer the same Saburo I once was."

Jojima look at him questioningly.

"I have been born again and changed."

Jojima looked intently at Saburo. Saburo smiled back at him.

"I have come to believe in Jesus Christ. I've become a Christian."

Face to Face With the Betrayer · 161

Jojima's eyes flew open.

"Mr. Jojima. Let's forget the past, OK?"

"What?" Jojima let out the muffled sound in surprise.

Saburo looked directly into Jojima's eyes. "I do not have any ill feelings toward you."

Jojima's eyes brimmed with tears and quickly overflowed. Saburo extended his hand. The other man grasped it tightly with both of his own.

"I'm sorry! Please, Saburo, forgive me, forgive me!"

"I have forgiven you, Mr. Jojima." Saburo's voice choked with tears.

Jojima broke down, a forgiven man, sobbing out loud.

The heavy rain drenched both of them, and the strong wind buffeted them. Neither noticed.

"Jojima-san, I have repented of my sins before God, and I have resolved to dedicate my entire life to God. You must have suffered a lot too, didn't you?"

"Yes. I have. Besides, I've had an illness for a long time."

"Listen, I no longer hate you. Here is how I feel now. We all need to repent of our sins and be forgiven. We all can live under God's loving care. This is what I have been wanting to tell you for some time. And that I am a happy man today, by God's grace."

"Saburo-san . . ."

"Let's promise to be a support to each other from now on."

With that, the two men embraced, smiling through their tears. Any trace of revenge or hate had been cast aside.

Chapter 22

A Journey Without an Ending

In March 1956 Saburo graduated with a degree in theology and waited anxiously to be called to fill a position as a pastor. Deep within his heart he harbored some anxiety about the whole idea. Could someone with his background really be a pastor? One by one, his classmates had received calls to ministerial internships all over Japan and were already leaving the campus. But no call came for Saburo.

I guess it was futile, after all. He was deeply disappointed and brooded alone in his dorm room. All the painful events of the war, painful memories of the past, came flooding back. *I should have known it was all for nothing.* Saburo buried his head in his hands.

There was another reason for his discouragement. A friend had introduced him to a young woman, a nurse. Their friendship had developed into love—at least on Saburo's part. It was a spoken promise only, but they had agreed to marry. Yet, one day, this woman sent him a letter abruptly ending their relationship. For whatever reason, she clearly asked him not to see her or write her again.

The future seemed so uncertain. How was he to make a living? He would soon be thirty years old. What would he do with his life? Saburo sank deeper into discouragement. An inner voice began to whisper in his ear, *I really am nothing but a failure. It was a big mistake from the beginning to want to become a minister. I should have known myself better, especially after what I've done. It's hopeless after all. I'll give up thinking about becoming a minister. I should be able to find some business in Okinawa that will bring good money.*

No! That is not true!! Saburo came to himself. He was sure those whispers must have been the voice of Satan.

In the prison cell in the basement of Oahu Prison, he had prayed to God and made a vow. "Please let me out of this place, God. I dedicate my life to evangelizing Okinawa. I submit my entire life to You." And God had answered his prayer. No matter what, he must do what he had promised God. *But how am I to make a living?*

Saburo fervently prayed to God and left his future in His hands.

It wasn't long until a request came to the school for someone who would be willing to do self-supporting evangelism in Okayama. There would be no salary or other financial support provided by the church organization; all living expenses would be covered by selling Christian books and literature house to house, while at the same time spreading the teachings of Jesus Christ. Would Saburo be interested in this work? It was frontier evangelism in an area with no churches and few believers.

Am I able to handle this job? he asked himself. It would be difficult work, he knew. *God got me out of prison so that I could work for Him,* he thought. I'll give it a try.

It would be a difficult work he was told, but an elderly woman offered to look after him.

God got me out of prison so that I could evangelize. . . . I'll give it a shot.

With renewed courage Saburo made his way to Okayama. He took with him as many books as he could carry. He also had a U.S. government-surplus sleeping bag. An elderly woman offered to provide him a room and to look after his laundry. "Mr Arakaki," she told him, "I am old and cannot do any evangelism, but I will do anything for your work. Please work hard for the Lord, and do my portion too."

Saburo was touched by her warmhearted kindness. He began to work, carrying his load of books from house to house in rain or shine, finding his way in this strange area. As he walked, drenched with sweat, he claimed God's promise in Isaiah 43:19. " 'Behold . . . I will even make a road in the wilderness and rivers in the desert.' " This verse was both an encouragement and a goal.

Doing literature evangelism on foot in a rural area was not easy. Progress was slow. What he needed was a bicycle. He wrote a letter to Hawaii about his predicament, and soon twenty dollars came in the mail. It was from Pastor Shohei Miyake.

Saburo purchased a used bicycle. He carried his sleeping bag with him, traveling around the rural district on his bicycle and conducting literature evangelism. Under the blazing sun, Saburo pedaled his bicycle all across the countryside. Whenever he got thirsty he would stop to ask for a drink of water. Many villagers would open their doors to him and offer him the juicy local peaches that were in season. At night he would sleep outdoors in his sleeping bag, contending with the heat and mosquitoes.

The villagers quickly noticed Saburo's honest and gentle character, and many purchased the books he offered. With these people as a base, Saburo enthusiastically organized Bible study groups.

Early the next year, he received a letter from Professor Yamagata of Saniku Gakuin College. The professor wanted to stop by to see Saburo while on his way to Nagasaki for a meeting. Concern about how Saburo was getting along in his self-supporting work weighed heavily on Professor Yamagata's mind.

Professor Yamagata was very surprised when he arrived in Okayama. Saburo had organized Bible study groups at five different locations, with some groups numbering as many as twenty individuals. In less than a year, Saburo had gathered around him numerous persons who were honest seekers of the teachings of Jesus Christ. The professor was deeply moved by his work.

In March, Professor Yamagata brought some unexpected good news. "In a committee action at the church constituency meeting, an action was taken to call you to evangelize Okinawa. There is one condition. You will need to return to Saniku Gakuin for one additional semester of classes."

Saburo spontaneously clasped his hands and lifted his eyes heavenward. "God did not abandon me after all! In order to give me practical experience, He had me first come to Okayama. Thank You, Lord!"

New courage and hope for the future filled his heart.

* * * * *

"I left college for Okinawa in June of 1957, leaving from Harumi Pier in Tokyo," Pastor Arakaki told Miike at Haneda Airport as they awaited their flight to Okinawa.

"At that time, how long had it been since you had been home in Okinawa?"

"Let's see . . . I left for Tinian when I was eight years old. How many years would that have been? Twenty-three years, because I was thirty-one when I returned."

A boy, born in Okinawa, had left for Tinian alone. He became entrapped in the war between the United States and Japan while living on Saipan. Escaping the grasp of the suicide cliff, he crossed through the valley of the shadow of death, committed a crime of murder—twice—and came within a hair's breadth of being executed in Guam. Then in Hawaii, he met God.

Pastor Arakaki and the film crew had come to the conclusion of their trip tracing the miraculous experiences of his life. Their journey had covered more than six thousand miles (ten thousand kilometers) and had delved deep into the emotions of everyone involved.

"Pastor Arakaki, you must be worn out," said Miike, thanking him for agreeing to the trip and its burdens.

"Oh, no! I want to thank you," Pastor Arakaki reached out to shake Miike's hand.

One journey was coming to an end, but the journey—the path on which God had set his feet so many years before—would continue. In Okinawa, Saburo Arakaki would continue to follow his Lord who had delivered him from death row to be a minister of the gospel of Christ. That journey was not yet completed.

A Personal Testimony

The hill of Mabuni, on the southern end of the main island of Okinawa, was the land of ultimate sacrifice during the Battle of Okinawa. It is the site of the only World War II ground battle in Japan proper. There, both military and civilians, driven to desperate straits, came to a terrible and tragic end. Today, rows and rows of monuments stand as a memorial to these terrible events.

The sharp cliffs of coral limestone stand watch over the Kuroshio—the Japanese current—flowing to the south, and bright red bougainvillea blossoms slowly dance to the tempo of the sea breeze.

This sure looks a lot like the Marpi Cliffs in Saipan, thought Miike. Those who stood on the precipice of both cliffs, cornered by the battle fire that closed in on them, stood also at the precipice of life.

In April 1945, a formidable U.S. force of 1,300 warships, including 20 battleships and 19 aircraft carriers with 1,160 aircraft—a total force numbering 182,000 men—launched its assault on Okinawa with its 450,000 inhabitants.

The U.S. land operations began with a fierce air attack and naval bombardment, almost identical to the strategy in Saipan. The principal defense force for the island, the Japanese Thirty-second Army, was no match against the American attack. Its fighting strength was largely gone. From the start, the Japanese strategy was to delay the enemy from its final assault on the main Japanese islands. It became a slow war of attrition. Without any resistance, the U.S. forces made a bloodless landing on southern Okinawa from the west central shores north of Naha. Okinawans were thrust into the vortex of the horrible ground battle.

The Japanese Thirty-second Army forces were positioned so that even with the loss of Shuri Castle, the key defensive position for Japanese resistance to the U.S. invasion, the fighting would continue. Imperial Headquarters had sent word to the local forces that "Okinawa is a vital part of the mainland and should be defended to the end." To defend against invasion of the mainland, Okinawa became the sacrifice, fighting until bitter defeat.

All adult males were drafted into the defense of Okinawa either as part of the regular military or as volunteers. High-school students, junior-high students, even females, were ordered to join in the defensive battle. Many of these died on the battlefield. Nearly 150,000 residents of Okinawa lost their lives. Some of these were killed by Japanese troops commandeering the caves in which they were hiding; others were driven to sacrifice their lives rather than surrender, and still others were killed by Japanese troops because they were suspected of being spies.

* * * * *

Upon his return to Okinawa, Saburo was fortunate enough to be reunited with his brother and sisters, who had somehow survived the war. However, Saburo's grandmother had died after she had been placed in a detention camp. His mother had escaped to the Kunigami Mountains in the north but had died from starvation. No remains had been preserved.

When Saburo returned in July 1957, Okinawa was still occupied by the U.S. military and was under U.S. administration. Okinawa would not be returned fully to Japan until twenty-seven years after the end of the war.

Having survived Saipan, the island of ultimate sacrifice, Saburo Arakaki returned to another island of ultimate sacrifice—Okinawa. He pondered the tragedy of countless lives snatched away in the war. *War is the slaughter of humanity under a country's flag. And it is the ultimate evil and sin by humanity against humanity. Why do human beings cause war and hate and fight each other? The cause is found deep in the human soul. And the cure must be the peace that comes to the soul through the love of Jesus Christ.*

" 'You have heard that it was said, "You shall love your neighbor and hate your enemy." But I say unto you, love your enemies, bless those who curse you, do good to them who hate you, and pray for those who spitefully use you and persecute you' " (Matthew 5:43, 44).

" 'Blessed are the peacemakers, For they shall be called sons of God' " (Matthew 5:9).

I want to spread this love that Christ teaches, Saburo thought. He had promised God that he would work to spread the gospel in Okinawa, and now he had returned. Following a one-month internship at the church in Shuri, he received a call to the gospel ministry to serve as a pioneer worker in Koza (now Okinawa City), a U.S. military town.

In September 1957, Saburo Arakaki married Yoshiko Matsudo at the Shuri church. In Yoshiko, he recognized the one God had selected for his life companion. Yoshiko's deep understanding, love, and dedication provided support for Saburo's work. The words of Paul in 2 Corinthians 13:4 were his daily guiding principle: "We shall live with Him [Jesus] by the power of God." Elder Shohei Miyake, who had been so instrumental in Saburo's transformation, attended the wedding ceremony, bringing fragrant orchids from Hawaii.

In September 1958, one year after Pastor Arakaki began his pioneer work in Koza, a woman who had begun studying the Bible asked that he visit her troubled home. Her husband, Mr. Takagi, had lost his job after suffering from tuberculous arthritis in his knee. He had lost strength in his legs and could not even stand on his own. He and his wife had three small children, and the family was living in despair and extreme poverty. Pastor Arakaki spoke to them about seeking God's grace. The couple began to read the Bible. Pastor Arakaki prayed fervently that Mr. Takagi's leg would be healed and that special blessings would be poured out on this family.

A light, although faint, began to flicker in that home. Soon Mr. Takagi began to express the desire to attend the Bible study meetings on Saturday. Of course, it was impossible for him to walk. Back then, there weren't any carriages, not to mention automobiles, so each Saturday Pastor Arakaki hoisted the forty-year-old man onto his back and carried him nearly a mile (one and a half kilometers) to the meetings! It didn't matter if the sun was blazing overhead or if it was pouring rain; Pastor Arakaki would faithfully carry the man to the meetings and back.

Even for a tough, sturdy man like Pastor Arakaki, the trip left him panting for breath and with sweat pouring down his forehead, stinging his eyes. The image of that pair—Mr. Takagi hoisted on Pastor Arakaki's back—touched the hearts of the many people who saw it each week.

Ten months elapsed. Mr. Takagi still had to crawl around on the floor of his house.

"Let's pray that you can walk," Pastor Arakaki insisted.

Together with the pastor, Mr. and Mrs. Takagi prayed fervently to God. When the last prayer had been said, Pastor Arakaki spoke directly to Mr. Takagi, "Stand up, Mr. Takagi. Go on. Stand up." Mr. Takagi, clutching at a pillar for support, stood. Spreading both arms out like wings, he slowly took a step forward, then another, his body swaying. With one step firmly planted, he stepped forward again and again. He walked!

"Oh, thank You, God! Lord, thank You!" his wife shouted, both hands clasped together as in prayer. Her eyes were brimming with tears.

The meeting place continued to be filled with new seekers for truth. Finally it became evident that a church building would be necessary to accommodate all of the believers. Pastor Arakaki threw himself wholeheartedly into the new building project. Pastor Arakaki's enthusiasm impressed the American Christians on the U.S. base, even Air Force Colonel Vogovich, who personally began fundraising for the building project within the base.

As soon as the site for the new church building had been finalized, Chaplain Mall, a Marine Corps chaplain, arrived with five men and two bulldozers, offering to prepare the site for construction.

In June 1960, the Koza church was completed. On the day of the church dedication service, Mr. Takagi arrived, walking on his own feet with the aid of crutches. It was a moving sight.

Pastor Arakaki also evangelized in remote, frontier areas, in addition to pastoring churches in a small town in the northern reaches of Okinawa and on another isolated island. After establishing the Koza church, he established churches in Itoman, Nago, Oroku, and Urasoe—a total of five churches. Countless men and women were baptized. On a single day in March 1967, twenty-five people were baptized on the seashore of Tsuken, a tiny, isolated island east of the main island. The remarkable, extraordinary work of the pastor began to be noted by many. Some called him the "Paul of Okinawa," a reference to the biblical Paul who worked so hard and faithfully building up churches and preaching the gospel following his conversion to Jesus Christ.

* * * * *

It was Saturday morning, and as always the church service was held in the home church of Pastor Arakaki in Uyebara in Naha City. About forty church members and nonmembers, children and elderly alike, had gathered in the worship room. Miike observed the service from the pew in the last row.

The worship began with hymns and singing, accompanied by Yoshiko Arakaki on the piano. Prayer followed. Then Pastor Arakaki stood at the pulpit and began to speak about the trip he and the film crew had taken to Saipan, Guam, and Hawaii.

"When I was asked to retrace the places where I had committed murder, where I spent hours in terror of impending death by execution, and where I was held in a prison cell, the place where I first encountered God's holy Word, and where I first experienced the salvation of Jesus Christ . . . when I was asked by Mr. Miike, who is sitting here, to take a trip retracing all of this, I honestly hesitated. I wondered why."

Miike stiffened. He recalled the day he had first met Pastor Arakaki and the tense look on the pastor's face as he was reminded of his bitter experience. He remembered, too, how the pastor's eyes had filled with pain on Saipan, when he stood at the spot where he had committed murder. Miike remembered how he had questioned in his heart why he had brought this man to relive this experience and how his own heart had become filled with an indescribable emotion followed by a deluge of tears.

As the believers listened intently, Pastor Arakaki deliberately and slowly raised one arm upward and swiftly brought it down emphatically, declaring, "I understood then that this was God's will for me."

For an instant Miike could not believe what he had just heard.

"I had a sense of awe and reverence," Pastor Arakaki continued. "My heart lifted heavenward. I entrusted everything into God's hands and began the trip. It was a very difficult trip, but people were so helpful everywhere we went, and everything went smoothly. When the way seemed closed, someone would appear to offer help. God sent us assistance. We thank Him for His guidance and His blessings."

"There is no such thing as 'coincidence' in the Bible," Pastor Arakaki had stated on the way home from Hawaii. Miike was suddenly struck by an epiphany—miracles do not happen by chance!

"The Bible teaches us truth," the pastor said. "It says in Proverbs 16, 'Commit your works to the Lord, and your thoughts will be established.' Also it says, 'A man's heart plans his way, but the Lord directs his steps.'

"As I went on the trip, I stood again on the very spot where I had committed a terrible sin. Once again, I asked the Lord to forgive me. And I renewed my covenant with the Lord, rededicating myself to carry the good news of His salvation."

As Miike listened to Pastor Arakaki speak, he thought of the words of Dr. Toshio Yamagata, professor emeritus at Saniku Gakuin College: "From convict on death row to preacher—this is a modern miracle. It is God's miracle of grace within human hearts."

To find the significant power that operates in Saburo Arakaki's life, I witnessed God's miraculous grace, Miike thought. The trip had turned out to be a testimony of God's grace.

Early that afternoon, a chorus of hymns filtered through the air along the beach of Senaga Island near the suburb of Naha City as the church celebrated a baptismal service. Shafts of golden sunshine penetrated the clouds, and the surface of the sea glistened in gold. A steady flow of waves bathed the white sand of the beach. Believers surrounded Pastor Arakaki and the three baptismal candidates wrapped in their black gowns.

From a safe distance in the shade of ironwood trees, Director Imura captured the scene using a telephoto lens. Over the shoulders of those gathered there, Miike watched as Pastor Arakaki led a woman into the water. In the golden light reflecting off the waves, the two figures in black gowns were silhouettes. Each rippling wave became a sparkling crystal, as the two descended waist-deep, then chest-deep into the crystalline sea, and faced each other. The pastor raised his right hand toward heaven.

"My beloved Sister Mitsuko Yara, by the faith you express in the Lord Jesus Christ, I, as a minister of the gospel of Jesus Christ, baptize you in the name of the Father, the Son, and the Holy Spirit. Amen."

Slowly the black form tilted backward, and the woman was buried in the shining sea.

Every sound, including that of the waves and distant cicadas, faded from Miike's ears. Something warm filled his heart.

Pastor Arakaki stood tall again, and the woman was resurrected from among the waves. Water trickled down from the black silhouettes. The droplets of water sparkled momentarily in small rainbow colors.

Almost reflexively, Miike exhaled deeply and turned his face upward toward heaven.

The sky was glowing, and the sound of voices singing hymns filled the air.

(Afterword to the Mainichi Newspapers Company edition, 1998)

In my hand I hold a copy of a clipping from the June 4, 1987, evening edition of the Mainichi newspaper published by the Western Japan Section of Mainichi News. It is a tiny article titled, "Former Death Row Convict Pastor Arakaki Preaches On." If I had not happened to notice this small article while staying in a hotel in Fukuoka City on a business trip, I most probably would not have written this documentary nonfiction book.[1] Is it some sort of fulfilled destiny that this book was published in Japanese by the Mainichi Newspapers Company?

I am greatly indebted to KBC Kyushu Asahi Broadcasting Company for providing the privilege of being able to retrace the journey of Pastor Saburo Arakaki. The trip itinerary was largely conceived by producer Jun Eto, who skillfully put it all together as a documentary that was broadcast on more than ten Asahi Television affiliated stations in Japan. I would like to express my sincere appreciation to all involved.

* * * * *

When I accompanied Pastor Arakaki to Saipan, Guam, and Hawaii, I limited my role to that of a listener and commentator, and not as a writer. The documentary, "Testament—A Confessional Trip," was the work of Producer Eto, who presented it as a nonnarrative work that, when completed, was a quiet, restrained, dignified piece. I received numerous telephone calls and letters in reaction to the broadcast from viewers who expressed how they had been deeply moved by the documentary.

However, some felt that they wanted to hear my narrative, my personal commentary. I sensed a need to someday write about what I had seen, heard, thought, and felt during my trip with Pastor Saburo Arakaki.

"You must write." It was like a voice from heaven. But progress in writing was not easy. One reason was that after completing the trip, several unusual happenings occurred, one after another, that caused me to become involved in time-consuming projects. While seemingly a digression, I will try to briefly explain some of these.

On the day that we were to leave Honolulu to fly home to Japan, Pastor Kojiro Matsunami offered to take us by car to the airport. On the way, we stopped by to see the Pacific National Memorial Cemetery located on top of the Punchbowl.

We had very little time left, so we managed to drive only around the perimeter of the Punchbowl. A large number of people were gathered near the center of the cemetery. Pastor Matsunami pointed to the grave where the people were and said, "That grave was erected for Mr. Onizuka, who died in the space shuttle Challenger accident."

In January of the previous year, Ellison Onizuka, a third-generation Japanese-American astronaut who was born in Hawaii, was scattered in the blue sky above Florida as a result of the tragic explosion of the space shuttle.

I had a strong urge to go down to his grave, but there was absolutely no time. As we were about to leave the cemetery, I unexpectedly blurted out, "Pastor Matsunami, I'll be back again next year." It wasn't something I had even thought about at that time. But the following year, in May 1988, I found myself standing in front of Ellison Onizuka's grave. I had been commissioned by TV Tokyo to write a documentary drama, "Astronaut Ellison Onizuka and his Mother." Plus, Kodansha Publishing Company had asked me to write the story of Onizuka, "Fly Toward Your Dreams."

Incidentally, Ellison was raised by parents who were firm in their religious upbringing, and he was himself a devout Buddhist, even serving as president of Hawaii's Young Buddhist Association. On that fateful day, Ellison was launched into space with a dream, and he wore a Hongwanji Temple pendant.

It was the following year that I had received a request from SBC, Shinetsu Broadcasting Company of Nagano, to write a documentary. More than forty years before, several photographs had been dedicated in a consecration service at a shrine in Okaya City, with prayers for the safe return of the men who went to the battlefront during the war. The documentary was to show the return of these dedicated photographs to the families. Some of these men had indeed returned alive from the war, but there were also those who never returned. When I was presented with the case of a person from Utsunomiya City who was convicted as a war criminal and executed, something flashed in the back of my mind.

"Utsunomiya . . . ? That person is . . . wasn't he an army physician?"

"Yes, he was," answered the production director.

"Was he sentenced and executed in Guam?"

"Yes, he was."

"Commander U?"

"Why yes . . . that's right!" The faces of the staff and especially, the news production director changed visibly. "How," he asked, "do you know all these details?"

I felt a strange feeling overpower me.

The visit by Pastor Arakaki and myself, along with a camera crew, to the site of the war crimes prison, had been widely reported in the local newspapers in Guam and even in Hawaii. When we arrived in Honolulu, we received a telephone call from an American journalist asking to see us. When we met, he spread out several dozen photographs on the table before us. They were detailed photographs of individuals sentenced to death—just prior to and immediately after their execution. Some of the photos appeared extremely cruel and merciless, and I found it impossible to even look at them directly.

Basically, since I was writing a documentary of the execution of war criminals in Guam and most likely would want such photographs, he was willing to offer them to me for a price. I had to tell him that, at this time, we did not need such photographs. As we turned to leave, he stopped me. "Here is something I wrote that I want you to have." He produced a tabloid newspaper called Islanders, and handed it to me. I thanked him and accepted it.

It was a special edition regarding the execution of Commander U, a navy physician, who was convicted and executed for responsibility in the murder of prisoners of war in Guam.

It wasn't until during our flight from Honolulu that I had a chance to read the articles. I was overwhelmed, and my heart trembled as I read Commander U's last will and testament written in poetic form to his wife and child in Utsunomiya.

When I heard of Utsunomiya during my briefing with SBC, I was instantly reminded of the incident. Could this be explained away as being just a coincidence? I felt that this was something beyond just a chance happening—a coincidence or an accident.

Commander U, a physician, was the medical director of the naval hospital on the island of Truk. He was executed in Guam near the end of March 1950—executed by hanging after being found responsible for the murder and death of war prisoners, although he had not issued any such orders.

SBC's director had requested interviews with the survivors of Commander U, but had been refused. I was asked to present the request again, to see if we could work something out.

Striking out in all directions, I first searched for the Japanese lawyer who had been assigned to defend Commander U in the military court in Guam. I visited the legal offices of the Military Court of Justice in Toranomon, Tokyo. There I met Lawyer K, who was surprised that I had identified him. He showed me the trial documents and explained how the trial had proceeded down to the execution.

At the end of our meeting, I asked Lawyer K, "Wasn't Dr. U a Christian?" The lawyer tilted his head slightly and said, "No, I don't think so." My guess had been wrong.

Dr. U's son was the same as age as me. I explained to him what was on my heart.

After his military service had ended, Dr. U reopened his family clinic. It was two years later, on a day with heavy snow, that U.S. military police arrested him on his doorstep as he returned from making house calls. The suffering of his family continued through many years filled with difficulties and sadness.

After our meeting, a family council was held, and the family decided that Dr. U's wife would meet with me—once, at any rate—to listen to what I had to say.

I visited the home of the late Dr. U in Utsunomiya. In the living room was a photograph of the doctor in full navy dress. Around the frame hung something that surprised me. A rosary.

"Was your husband a Christian?"

"Yes. Just before the execution, I understand he was baptized by the priest." The aged woman then brought out a red velvet object the size of a small book, and removing the rosary from the frame, she placed both on the table in front of me. The red velvet was folded into thirds, and when it was opened, I could see a small silver cross, fastened by a thread in the center of the velvet.

"My husband made this cross from the silver foil of cigarette boxes. It seems that when he prayed, he stood this three-fold velvet on its edge in front of him and prayed. His hopes were strengthened by the cross, and he probably was seeking God's saving grace."

The wife stared at the rosary in her hands. "This is the rosary that was hanging on his neck when he climbed the scaffold for the execution. The priest told me of those last moments."

Later on I had the opportunity to meet Priest T in Yokohama. The priest had conducted the baptism at the request of Commander U, and on the very next day he also accompanied him to the scaffold.

In Guam, just as Pastor Arakaki had mentioned, executions took place away from the prison. They were performed inside a large Quonset building that stood at the end of the road and was approached by driving up a hill by car.

Commander U, the naval physician, in his last words to the priest, asked, "Will I be able to go to my wife and child?"

"Most certainly you can go, and you will go." Upon hearing these words the commander nodded with a quiet smile.

"Thank you for your kind care. I will be going ahead now."

The commander graciously bowed his head to express his thanks, and with light steps he ascended the thirteen steps to the scaffold.

I visited his grave and prayed for his repose and peaceful rest. A Christian name was written on the tombstone, which was engraved with a cross.

With the understanding and cooperation of the U family, the SBC documentary "My Father, My Husband, Went to War: The Testimony of Long-Preserved Photographs" was produced and broadcast. The broadcast, containing poems of life he left for his children, touched the hearts of many viewers. It told of an unfortunate, senseless death due to war.

After the broadcast I received a letter from his son saying he felt that now his father had returned home at last.

* * * * *

As I tried to write the miraculous life of Pastor Saburo Arakaki, the writing did not proceed as smoothly as I wanted, although I had a strong impression of a God-given duty to write the story.

One reason was that I felt that it was beyond my writing ability. How do you portray in words the horrifying events—the unendurable pain, the extreme terror of being killed—that drove this person to the desperate ultimate sacrifice of life for the honor of Japan? It was far beyond the limits and capability of my imaginative powers.

Another reason was that for several years I had been absorbed in the writing and movie production, and eventually stage drama production, of *Summer of Moonlight Sonata,* a documentary novel that portrayed the sacrifices of special attack missions, the Kamikaze, during the last period of the war.

Ten years had passed since the conception of this new project, "Rainbow Over Hell." This seems like a long time, but every chance I had, I continued to work on the documentary and looked forward to the opportunities I had to meet with Pastor Arakaki for interviews.

In addition, writing this documentary required the study of the Bible.

The production of the movie and then the stage drama demanded an exceptionally arduous work schedule that left me physically exhausted, and my physician ordered a complete rest, after which I again resumed writing.

But I still sensed being overwhelmed and beset by seemingly endless difficulties. I seemed to be making only slow progress—if any—toward my ever-distant destination.

Finally, on December 7, 1997, I was suddenly awakened before daybreak by what I thought was a strong knocking on my door. "You must awaken!" it seemed to say, and I knew in my heart what I should be doing. I felt that I must repent of the way I had been approaching this project and that, without further hesitation or procrastination, I had to write about the testimonial journey.

I began by discarding all of what I had previously written. I had to begin again from the very first sentence.

I wrote during the day and continued at night. I did not even rest for the year-end activities or the New Year's holiday. And amazingly, within seventy days I completed writing *Rainbow Over Hell.*

As I was writing the final chapter, Pastor Arakaki and his wife were about to leave for the United States for a lecture tour. I immediately sent copies of the first six chapters of the manuscript to Okinawa, requesting him to check them for accuracy.

Pastor Arakaki telephoned me immediately after reading the paragraphs describing the banzai charge in Saipan when he was hiding out in the mountain jungle. He exclaimed, "I was surprised! It was exactly as written. It was as though you had actually been there right by my side. It's amazing that you were able to write like that. I cannot but think that the Holy Spirit was speaking through you."

I dare not deny it. As I faced the word processor, I felt that somehow I was controlled by the will of a higher power as I wrote.

I know of no other case in the world in which a war criminal sentenced to death became a pastor. Pastor Arakaki's experience is a singular, unprecedented miraculous event in the world.

His former teacher Dr. Toshio Yamagata (former president of Saniku Gakuin College, Honorary Doctor of LL.D. from Andrews University in the United States) has on several occasions said to me, "Saburo Arakaki is a person with a pure heart and unquestionable integrity. He has a true and deep love for the souls of individuals."

In his preface to From Ex-Convict on Death Row to Minister, a collection of lectures by Pastor Arakaki, Dr. Yamagata stated:

[Pastor Arakaki] is fearless for his Lord. But on the other hand he is a very gentle and kind person. He has the ability to sense the needs and feelings of others and acts considerately. One may draw an incorrect impression merely from his outward appearance. And he is polite and courteous in his actions.

He is without question a vessel that God is using at a time when the world is faced with unprecedented problems without any certainty of having solutions. As I think of that young man in death row studying his Bible, and see the result of God's marvelous act of intervening love, I am deeply moved and can only give Him praise. From death row convict to minister of God—truly a modern day miracle! It is the miracle of change that occurs in the hearts of men and women through the marvelous grace of God.

The friendship between former Military Police Officer Jojima and Pastor Arakaki continues to this day. Pastor Arakaki has invited Mr. Jojima to Okinawa, where he has even assisted in the pastor's work.

After the war, Mr. Jojima visited Saipan on many occasions, endeavoring to collect the remains of the war dead who sleep in the jungles and the numerous caves.

Pastor Arakaki reached retirement age and retired from church work at sixty-three. However, he continues to spread the gospel message, lecturing widely in Japan and also abroad in the United States, Canada, Korea, and elsewhere.

On June 5, 1998, soon after Pastor and Mrs. Arakaki returned from a lecture tour to the United States, Yoshiko, Saburo's dedicated wife, passed away due to heart failure and now rests in sleep. She had been granted sixty-seven years of life. Her funeral was held on June 7 in the Naha Seventh-day Adventist Church.

Mysteriously, on this beautiful watery planet called Earth, a planet that nurses life, humans perpetuate a history of struggle and war. In the twentieth century humanity has twice repeated world wars in a desperate, mad rush of massacre and destruction resulting in poverty, famine, abhorrent murders, and the terror of inevitable death. But in all this, there is something about the story of Saburo Arakaki that is rich in implications for something better, something that sheds light on this world's strife and confusion.

Trapped on the edge of Marpi's "Suicide Cliff" in the battle of Saipan, Saburo saw, rising amid a sea of the smoke of battle, a rainbow. In every hellish ordeal, I would like to think that surely somewhere, a rainbow is shining forth with the light of the hope of salvation and true peace for humanity.

In all the insecurity that floods human hearts in the twenty-first century, as humanity stands pregnant with the possibility of heading toward imminent destruction, let us search for that rainbow. My prayer is that Pastor Arakaki's miraculous life will be a message of hope, filled with the light of love, to everyone who hears it.

Several sources, including the following, have been used for reference materials in the production of this book. I would like to express my appreciation for these sources.

1. In Defense Agency, National Defense College, War History Room, War History Collection: "Strategies for Army Forces in the Central Pacific Region"; Until the Marianas Suicide; and Army Strategies for the Okinawa Area. Asagumo Shimbunsha.

2. Shirai Bungo (ed.) *Retsujitsu Saipan* (Intensely Hot Saipan), Tokyo News Publishing Co.

3. Nomura Susumu, *The Mother Country Yonder Over the Sea,* Jiji News Agency.

4. Collection of transcripts of lectures by Pastor Saburo Arakaki, From *Ex-Convict on Death Row to Minister;* Hiroshima Saniku Gakuin.

I have faithfully and honestly documented facts as they were, using actual names where possible for actual persons. However, by necessity, fictitious names or initials were used in some cases.

I was extremely fortunate to have this documentary published by the Mainichi Newspapers, to whom I was introduced by Mr. Moriyuki Torii, my senior, whom I would like to thank.

I would like to express my deep appreciation for the efforts of Mr. Susumu Yamamoto, director of publishing; Mr. Hajime Kitamura, chief literary editor; and Mr. Kazuo Shima, who was in charge of the editorial work.

Needless to say, it would have been impossible to accomplish this project, first and foremost, without the cooperation of Pastor Saburo Arakaki and his much-needed, constant encouragement. I am indebted as well to the many individuals without whose combined strengths this book could never have been written.

With heartfelt gratitude to God, I dedicate this book to Pastor Saburo Arakaki and to the late Mrs. Yoshiko Arakaki who supported her husband for forty-one years.

Tsuneyuki Mohri
June 1998

[1]I am "Yasufumi Miike" who accompanied Pastor Arakaki and the film crew throughout the retracing of the miraculous events in his life as told in *Rainbow Over Hell*. I use this name in the book in order to maintain a certain amount of objectivity in the telling of the story.

Postscript 2: Changed Lives

(Kodansha Publishing edition, 2005)

For me, *Rainbow Over Hell* is a mysterious creation. Since the publication of the first Japanese edition (Mainichi Newspapers Company, 1998), some unanticipated and astonishing events have taken place. Let me take this opportunity to share some of these.

In the postscript to the first edition, I wrote the following: " 'You must write.' It was like a voice from heaven. . . . I felt that somehow I was controlled by the will of a higher power as I wrote." That was truly how I felt.

Disallowing all fictitious elements, I depicted only what really happened, traveling to the actual sites that had led a man on a path from death row convict to pastor.

For the young Saburo Arakaki, being introduced to the Bible called forth a beam of light, like sunlight through the trees, to shine into his heart hardened with anguish and despair. It was the light of salvation, the light of hope. Even in the circumstances of a "living hell," there is always a rainbow, somewhere, that shines with the light of hope.

Perhaps after reading this book, some individuals will want to read the Bible. That has been my unspoken feeling, although I, myself, have limited knowledge of the Bible. The reality has exceeded my expectations.

Apparently, some readers have been so moved by this story that they decided to be baptized—according to a phone call I received from Pastor Saburo Arakaki. And not just one person. I was astonished. In addition, Arakaki's story had quietly begun to create ripples in Japanese-American circles on the West Coast of the United States.

On December 26, 1997, Pastor Arakaki was invited to the Westminster church in Orange County, California (pastored by Yorito Uyeda), where Mr. Tamotsu Tanaka and four others were baptized.

After that, something even more astonishing occurred. I have mentioned this in the afterword for a sister volume called *Never Lose Your Smile* (Mainichi Newspapers Company) and also in the afterword for *Sea of Moonlight* (Kodansha Publishing), but let me share it anew here.

In the midst of a serious financial recession in Japan, the computer software company that Yoshio Suzuki managed in Nagoya was headed toward bankruptcy. Rather than cause his creditors difficulty, he thought to settle these debts with his own life insurance money. On January 5, 1999, he headed to Los Angeles, where he intended to commit suicide.

Because of some mix-up, he was unable to stay at the hotel at which he had made reservations, and so it happened that he came to stay at the Better Living Center, managed by Pastor Shinsei Hokama. Concerned by the despondent look on Mr. Suzuki's face, Pastor Hokama's wife, Hisako, recommended that he read a Japanese copy of *Rainbow Over Hell*. Mr. Suzuki read it in one sitting and wept.

The next day, Pastor Saburo Arakaki arrived at the Better Living Center following another baptismal ceremony at the Westminster church, and thus, Mr. Suzuki unexpectedly met the main character of the book he had just read. He was moved by Pastor Arakaki's words and felt that there must be a God. Yet, he still thought that God was not interested in him or his problems. That evening, he tried to kill himself with poison.

However, for some unknown reason, he did not die. Late that night, he opened up his heart to an acquaintance who happened to drop by. Mr. Suzuki told him that he wanted to die, taking all his worries with him.

"Don't give up! Be strong and live!" his acquaintance urged. Even as he was considering death, here was someone telling him not to die. Suddenly, Mr. Suzuki recalls, he felt the power of God's presence like a punch in the stomach. *I didn't die. God has made me live,* he thought.

Since he had come to stay at the Better Living Center, mysterious coincidences had happened one after another. Were they miracles? Words from

Rainbow Over Hell rang in his mind—"There is no such word as 'coincidence' in the Bible" and "Miracles do not happen by chance." He felt strongly that this was all a part of God's plan.

Pastor Arakaki urged him to commit to starting his life anew. So Mr. Suzuki returned to Japan and called me to share the whole story.

"Now," Mr. Suzuki said, "I feel God's presence in my life."

His company went bankrupt, but Mr. Suzuki felt that his life had dramatically changed course, and he started a new life.

Hearing his extraordinary story, many people began to ask counsel of Mr. Suzuki. In the midst of seemingly endless despair and serious crises during the critical economic downturn in Japan, many were seeking reprieve from their anguish. Mr. Suzuki wanted all of them to be able to hear Pastor Arakaki's story. He thought that it would be a great encouragement to them, and so he launched a plan for Pastor Arakaki to speak at a public lecture hall.

About two hundred people gathered for Pastor Arakaki's talk in a conference hall for small businesses near JR Nagoya Station in Aichi Prefecture. I accepted an invitation to attend this meeting. As soon as I stepped into the room, a couple of individuals who were taking care of an elderly woman in a wheelchair said to me, "This lady was baptized because of *Rainbow Over Hell*."

I was astonished, but it did not end there. After the meeting, another woman walking with a cane came to tell me that she had been baptized because of reading *Rainbow Over Hell*.

These days, Mr. Suzuki works as manager of Daichi Home ("Home on Earth") a day service for severely handicapped individuals in Nagoya City.

There are numerous stories of others who experienced dramatic life changes after reading this book. One man said that he had read *Rainbow Over Hell* just before he was going to travel to Ishigakijima in Okinawa to pay the ultimate price for a life wracked with remorse, self-condemnation, and guilt for many long years after the war. Because of this book, he turned away from the journey that was to end in suicide. He had been a commanding officer in the Japanese air force who had failed in completing his

Kamikaze mission and had survived. In his story, I felt a revelation of divine power that far surpasses human intellect.

This book was born, I believe, through the urging of some great divine power.

The Christian writer Ayako Miura read *Rainbow Over Hell* and wrote to me while she was still living. "I believe," she wrote, "that God allowed you to write this literary work." I am filled with gratitude.

I believe that if this book brings something to people struggling with suffering, sadness, or worry, it is not through the power of what I have written but, rather, through light from God and His love.

Interest in Pastor Saburo Arakaki's amazing life has been spreading in the world. In June 1999, "Rainbow Over Hell: The Story of Pastor Saburo Arakaki" was the cover story of the World Edition of the *Adventist Review,* a weekly Protestant Christian publication, and thus its influence spread internationally.

Pastor Arakaki has received invitations to evangelize throughout Japan and also in Korea, and in many parts of the United States, including California, Kentucky, Minnesota, and Washington.

In Okinawa, a monthly gathering called The Seven Colors of the Rainbow Assembly was born. It included Pastor Arakaki and consisted of people who were moved by the reading of *Rainbow Over Hell*. Attendees traveled from as far away as Iwate Prefecture and Aichi Prefecture to be a part of the gathering.

In Brazil, *Rainbow Over Hell* has been serialized in a daily Japanese-language paper, *Nikkei Shimbun,* in São Paulo. And now, the English translation by Sharon Fujimoto-Johnson has been realized in the United States.

In 2005, Pastor Saburo Arakaki turned seventy-nine years old. That year also marked the sixtieth anniversary of the end of World War II. I'm pleased that this story will become part of Kodansha's collection of books. I'm thankful for the efforts of Masanobu Makita and kindness of the publishing department at Kodansha.

I'm grateful that this book will become available to more readers around the world.

"Humans cannot escape facing the sufferings of hell," says the founder of the Jodo Shinshu sect of Buddhism. When faced with hell-like trials, how do human beings find the path to life? Where do they seek the light that will illuminate the path before them? In the twenty-first century the world faces new crises in war, and humanity continues to face uncertainty and suffering. My unceasing prayer is that the message in Saburo Arakaki's amazing story will place over each of us—with our burdens of suffering—a rainbow of hope that transcends doctrines and belief systems.

With a prayer for true peace in the world,
Tsuneyuki Mohri
Constitution Memorial Day in Japan, May 2005

Translator's Note

When I read *Jigoku-no-Niji (Rainbow Over Hell)* in Japanese for the first time, it unfolded before my eyes like a movie full of drama, suspense, action, and emotion. In fact, if it had been fiction, I would have called it too fantastic to be believable. But Saburo Arakaki's story is true; it is a war documentary, a conversion testimony, a survival story, a tale of tragedy and triumph, all in one.

The theme of betrayal and forgiveness lingered in my thoughts for days. At first I commiserated with Saburo, who raged with anger at MP Corporal Jojima for betraying his trust. Then I was promptly astonished at the transformation of Saburo's heart and at his absolute, all-encompassing forgiveness of the man who had betrayed him.

Popular culture reinforces our desire to take revenge—"an eye for an eye, a tooth for a tooth." We want the one who has been wronged to rise up and triumph over the antagonist. We cheer when the bad guy is dragged down to his final end, because wrong must be avenged.

In *Rainbow Over Hell,* the revenge rule was broken by Saburo's act of forgiveness toward his undeserving betrayer. At the moment when we most expect and want Saburo to face off with Jojima, we are instead melted by forgiveness. It is a revelation of Saburo's true character, a heart undeniably changed by divine power. Believing that he himself had been forgiven by God, Saburo, in turn, forgave and succeeded in breaking the cycle of hatred and revenge that leads humans to war against each other time and again. Saburo was a mirror of God's forgiveness.

I have always believed in God. What changed in my heart during the translation of *Rainbow Over Hell* was that I realized God believes in us. As He believed in Saburo Arakaki and saw a man of God and not a murderer, so He believes in us. Even when we do not yet believe in Him. Even when we perhaps do not deserve to be believed in. In that way, He has hung a rainbow over each of our individual peaks of despair.

Sharon Fujimoto-Johnson

Translator

Author's Biography

Tsuneyuki Mohri. Author, Playwright. Born in 1933 in Fukuoka Prefecture, Japan. Graduated from the Department of Law and Literature of Kumamoto University. His television drama "The Eighteenth Year Draft," written in 1964, was awarded the first Kubota Mantaro Award. His book *Summer of Moonlight Sonata* (Chohbunsha, Kodansha Publishing Company), a behind-the-scenes portrayal of the Kamikaze, became a hit movie in 1993, which was viewed by over two million. In addition he has written *Never Lose Your Smile* (Mainichi Newspapers Company), *Fly Toward Your Dream—The Story of Astronaut Ellison Onizuka* (Kodansha Publishing Company), and other books.

If you enjoyed this book, you'll enjoy these as well:

Red Star Rising

Sunshine Siu Stahl as told to Kay D. Rizzo. Shao Zhao Yang's extraordinary vocal talent propelled her to fame as an opera star in Communist China. Though she considered herself a Seventh-day Adventist Christian, on stage she could forget her Adventist upbringing and the public humiliation and persecution her family endured at the hands of Chairman Mao's Red Guards. The memories of her name change, family exile, and "denunciation meetings" made her grateful for her new life of stardom. But what of her faith? Could she ever really forget?

0-8163-2122-1. Paperback.
US$13.99, Can$18.99

Shot Down!

John Curnow. When he lied about his age and joined the Royal Air Force at age 17, John Curnow didn't know that the life expectancy of an RAF crewman flying over enemy territory was calculated in weeks, not years. After his plane exploded, he suddenly found himself riding a parachute down to German-occupied France—the sole survivor among his crewmates. While God spared his life, it wasn't until nine years later, working as a tea plantation manager in India, that he gave his heart to God. This is a POW story you'll never forget.

0-8163-2109-4. Paperback.
US$15.99, Can$21.99

Prisoner for Christ

Stanley Maxwell. During the dark days of Communist China when Christians in Shanghai were persecuted by the government, Pastor Robert Huang went underground and continued his ministry. When he was finally arrested and sentenced without trial to a notorious prison, Robert's faith was put to the ultimate test.

0-8163-2054-3. Paperback.
US$13.99, Can$18.99.

Order from your ABC by calling **1-800-765-6955**, or get online and shop our virtual store at **www.adventistbookcenter.com**.
- Read a chapter from your favorite book
- Order online
- Sign up for email notices on new products

Prices subject to change without notice.